BENDY
AND THE INK MACHINE™

JOEY DREW STUDIOS™

EMPLOYEE HANDBOOK

BY CALA SPINNER

SCHOLASTIC INC.

Joey,

After much thought I have decided that it's time for me to move on from the studio. Let's discuss as soon as you have an opening on your schedule.

I hope you'll understand, old friend.

—Henry

Top five places I'd like to go to when I (finally) get out of town:
1. California
2. Athens
3. Rome
4. Giza
5. Anywhere but here—

Groceries to pick up:
- Bacon
- Red potatoes
- Onion
- Butter
- Ground black pepper
- Salt
- Dried parsley
- Milk

To-do list:
1. Finish preliminary sketches
2. Leave note for Joey
3. Clear out files
4. Have a nice, hot bath at home

DREAMS COME TRUE!

Welcome to

JOEY DREW STUDIOS™

Dreams

It all starts with a **DREAM**. The dream is the spark which sets the wheels in motion. You just have to believe that anything is possible. That's how all cartoons at Joey Drew Studios start.

Come

When we all **COME** together and work hard and happy, the impossible gets created. This is the part where everyone gets to play their role in turning dreams into realities we can all enjoy.

True

When our masterpiece is finished, we behold the new **TRUTH** we created. Our dreams are now a reality, and ready to share with everyone who wants to be happy.

Joey Drew

WORK
HARD
WORK
HAPPY

JOEY DREW STUDIOS™

Photos © Shutterstock: splatters throughout: (Anastacia-azzzya), (DigitalShards), (ESB Professional), (EVZ), (GriyoLabs), (iadams), (WitchEra), papers throughout: (Anelina), (Feng Yu), (Gosteva), (hidesy), (I. Pilon), (Karramba Production), (LiliGraphie), (nunosilvaphotography), (Picsfive), (Rudy Bagozzi), (showcake), (Valentin Agapov), 1 background texture and throughout (Lukasz Szwaj), 2 paperclip and throughout (AVS-Images), 2 envelope (Mark Carrel), 2 coffee spills and throughout (Juhku), 3 top right drips and throughout (Kirill. Veretennikov), 5 banner and throughout (bodabis), 5 texture and throughout (Milos Djapovic), 10 torn paper and throughout (s_oleg), 15 photo frame and throughout (Popartic), 15 tape and throughout (Odua Images), 16 texture and throughout (Bruno Ismael Silva Alves), 67 warranty paper (Artist_R), 67 receipt and throughout (Jill Battaglia), 83 cup ring (schankz), 114 papers (Mark Carrel), 148 push pin and throughout (Feng Yu), 167 splatters (xpixel).

10 9 8 7 6 5 4 3 2 1   19 20 21 22 23

ISBN 978-1-338-34392-2

Printed in the U.S.A. 40

First printing 2019

Book design by Amazing15

Featuring Artwork by Firion Bifrost, Prismahays, AtAt, WhicheverComa, Katie Guinn, Shannon Marie, NoisyPaperDragon, Nao Sasaki, MissPeya, Merkurfisch, Cary, Weretoons, TimTheHobo

Additional illustrations by Abby Bulmer

CO TENTS

Frame (00218)

Frame (00298)

Frame (00308)

Frame (00315)

Frame (00374)

Frame (00415)

Frame (00423)

Frame (00462)

Frame (00484)

Frame (00518)

Frame (00534)

Frame (00561)

Frame (00592)

Frame (00601)

Frame (00637)

PART I

SURVIVING YOUR FIRST WEEK

Congratulations on your recent employment with Joey Drew Studios! Now that you're officially part of the team, you'll want to know everything there is to know about working here. And why wouldn't you? It's the best place in the world to work!

In this section you'll discover some of the studio's state-of-the-art tools and facilities, as well as the cartoons you will be working on. In the weeks to come, hold fast to this helpful manual—it can be a real lifesaver!

We do what we can to cover all our bases in this employee manual, but as protocols and personnel change, feel free to add your own notes and updates to this guide. As you meet new people and learn new things, it can help to ask questions of your coworkers to make sure you have procedures down pat. A studio is only as strong as its weakest link, as Mister Drew likes to say, and an inquisitive mind leads to a better tomorrow!

CHAPTER ONE
"MOVING PICTURES"

DEAR HENRY,

IT SEEMS LIKE A LIFETIME SINCE WE WORKED ON CARTOONS TOGETHER.
30 YEARS REALLY SLIPS AWAY, DOESN'T IT?

IF YOU'RE BACK IN TOWN, COME VISIT THE OLD WORKSHOP.
THERE'S SOMETHING I NEED TO SHOW YOU.

YOUR BEST PAL, *Joey Drew*

Studio Layout

Joey Drew Studios has a sprawling campus, and it's growing bigger by the day! You can use this helpful map to navigate.

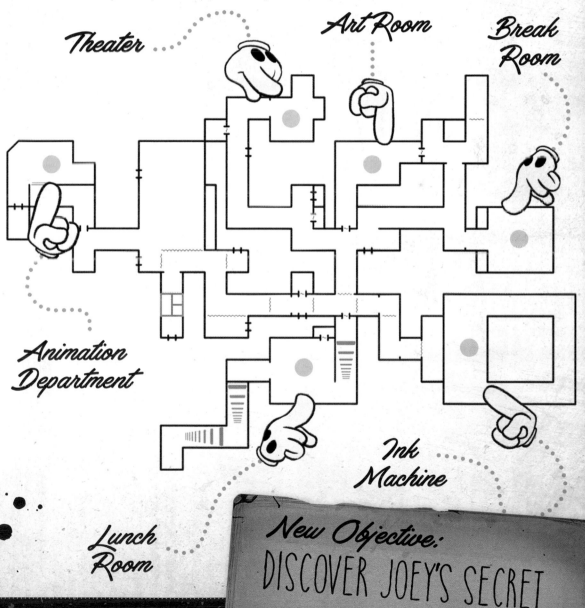

Theater

Art Room

Break Room

Animation Department

Ink Machine

Lunch Room

New Objective:
DISCOVER JOEY'S SECRET

From: Joey Drew

Memo to Staff Regarding the Ink Machine

People often ask me what sets Joey Drew Studios apart from your average Joe Schmoe Studios. Why, it's our wonderful staff, of course, but how can we take our work to the next level? I present to you ... the Ink Machine!

The Ink Machine is the latest in artistic technology, custom created in conjunction with the Gent Corporation just for us. This marvel of a machine churns out high-grade, fine-quality ink and pumps it throughout the studio like a steady, beating heart. This ink can be used not just for drawing, but also for creating usable, life-sized productions of, well, just about anything you can think of!

Why might we need our own Ink Machine, you ask? Excellent question! A gourmet chef doesn't use second-rate ingredients; no, she carefully selects the finest goose liver for her foie gras to avoid committing a faux pas. Actually I think foie gras is disgusting, so let's rephrase. Macaroni and cheese. Now what's better: Macaroni and cheese made with whatever cheese you can scrounge up at the corner deli, OR macaroni and cheese made from a blend of finely aged Gouda and Havarti?

Think of the Ink Machine as the vessel for your gourmet cheese blend. This ink can be placed into the newly installed "Ink Maker" machines around our studio, to print whatever you'd like—a wrench, a radio, a gear, a plunger, you name it! Because this ink is the crème de la crop in the ink world, it can also enable you to render illustrations so crisp, so real, you might think they could actually come to life. Can you imagine?

BEWARE THE INK MACHINE

Directions:

Search the decaying workshop. Along the way you may locate several items of interest.

- Bacon Soup: When your health is low, eating a can of Bacon Soup will instantly restore it.
- Audio Logs: These recordings were left by employees of the studio for you to listen to.
- Radio: Each chapter contains a radio you can turn on and listen to. You might even recognize some of the songs!
- Punch Card Stand: Punching in saves your progress.

Follow the overhead signs until you come to the Ink Machine Room. You will need to collect and insert two dry cells to power the lift. The batteries are located to your left, one inside the trunk and another on the shelf. Insert them into the power module to the right of the lever, then pull the lever to activate the lift.

New Objective:
FIX THE INK MACHINE

Now that you've activated the Ink Machine, you will need to repair it and turn it on. To repair it, head to the Power Station Room, where you'll learn you need to gather the following six items:

1. **GEAR:** Return to the Ink Machine Room and open the chest to the left of the doorway.

2. **BENDY DOLL:** Sitting on a chair in the Theater.

3. **BOOK:** Head downstairs to the Lunch Room to find *The Illusion of Living* on a table.

4. **INK JAR:** Back toward the entrance, find the ink jar on a desk beneath a "Work Hard, Work Happy" poster in the Animation Department. You can also spot a fun Easter egg at this desk—the animation cel on the desk changes each time you wander away from it.

5. **RECORD:** A light will turn off in the room containing the radio. Once it does, you'll be able to enter and retrieve the record from underneath the desk.

6. **WRENCH:** Inside the open chest of the life-sized Boris the Wolf.

To: Staff

Happy Holidays from Joey Drew Studios!

Another year at Joey Drew Studios has certainly brought us closer together! No one could have foreseen the many triumphs and challenges we've come upon this year, but one thing is for certain: We'll weather any hardship, and celebrate any victory, together.

In the spirit of the season, I'm asking each and every one of you to donate something from your work station—an object that means something to you and stands for who you are, the essence of what makes you, you. I've laid out some pedestals in the break room for you to leave them on. With any luck, we'll be able to appease the gods to bless us with another successful year.

Wishing you and yours a joyous holiday season to reflect on all you're thankful for.

Voice of
WALLY FRANKS

At this point, I don't get what Joey's plan is for this company. The animations sure aren't being finished on time anymore. And I certainly don't see why we need this machine. It's noisy, it's messy. And who needs that much ink anyway?

Also, get this, Joey had each one of us donate something from our work station. We put them on these little pedestals in the break room. To help appease the gods, Joey says. Keep things going.

I think he's lost his mind, but, hey, he writes the checks.

But I tell you what, if one more of these pipes burst, I'm outta here.

TOP SECRET

Interacting with the
Ink Machine

We're proud to have such advanced technology as the Ink Machine available in our studio, but be advised that this machine is both expensive and sensitive. Please refrain from interacting with the Ink Machine unless you have received express permission from our resident Gent repairman, Thomas Connor, or Mister Drew himself.

In the unlikely event of a burst pipe, ink pressure can be turned down or off completely using the pressure valve in the rear of the Theater. Subordinate valves throughout the studio can also help drain ink from a burst pipe, but should only be used in emergency situations. Please alert

our janitor, Wally Franks, to any ink spills, and tell staff to avoid the area until Mr. Franks can clean the mess.

Should you require ink, consult the weekly Ink Output Schedule that's posted for your convenience. Ink is piped directly to your work area, so you should not need to visit the Ink Machine itself for any reason outside an emergency.

New Objective:
TURN ON THE INK MACHINE

After placing all the objects on their respective pedestals, head to the Theater and turn the ink pressure valve. Then return to the Power Station and flip the switch.

Voice of
THOMAS CONNOR

It's dark and it's cold and it's stuck in behind every single wall now. In some places, I swear this godforsaken ink is clear up to my knees! Who ever thought that these crummy pipes could hold up under this kind of strain either knows something about pressure I don't, or he's some kind of idiot.

But the real worst part about all this . . . are them noises the system makes. Like a dying dog on its last legs. Make no mistake, this place . . . this . . . machine . . . heck, this whole darn thing . . . it just isn't natural.

You can bet, I won't be doing any more repair jobs for Mister Joey Drew.

OVERACHIEVER!

A few achievements will be given to you through the natural course of the story:

 PICKING UP THE PIECES: Collect all the pedestal items.

 HELLO BENDY: Fall through the floor.

But before you head to the Ink Machine Room to finish *Chapter 1: "Moving Pictures,"* be sure to check the following items off your to-do list:

 CROONER TUNER: Turn on the radio in the room where you found the record.

 THE CREATOR: To the right of the life-sized Boris the Wolf, walk straight through the wall containing the "Sheep Songs" poster to find a secret room and theMeatly.

 THE PAST SPEAKS: Listen to all the audio logs in this chapter. There are two: one from Wally Franks in the narrow room next to the closet, and one from Thomas Connor after you fall through the floor (after returning to the Ink Machine Room).

 THE TASTE OF HOME: Collect all the Bacon Soup in this chapter (see page 17).

STUDIO LAYOUT

BASEMENT

DELICIOUS!

BRIAR LABEL
BACON SOUP

Made from a traditional family recipe Briar Label Bacon Soup tastes just like the home kitchen cooking that mom used to make

"JUST THE WAY THE LITTLE DEVIL LIKES IT"

12 CENTS

THE TASTE OF HOME

There are twenty-one cans of Bacon Soup scattered throughout the studio in Chapter 1. Be sure to get them all for "The Taste of Home" achievement.

- One can, lower drawer of the dresser.
- One can, under the projector.
- Five cans, downstairs closet.
- One can, on a shelf to the left of a door.
- Four cans, in the closet beside Wally Franks's audio log.
- One can, inside the closet full of projectors.
- Three cans, on the shelves beyond the projector.
- One can, under the projector.
- Two cans, on the shelves to the right of the desk.

After falling through the floor . . .

- One can, bottom of the shelves containing Thomas Connor's audio log.
- One can, left of the transmutation circle in the Ritual Room. (Tip: Avoid the transmutation circle when walking into this room, or else you will trigger a cutscene.)

Bendy!

Allow us to introduce you to the mischievous little devil who started it all: Bendy! By now, we're certain you've noticed that Bendy is the face of Joey Drew Studios. A playful little fellow, Bendy can get up to some naughty antics when left to his own devices. Luckily he has friends like Boris the Wolf to keep him in check.

Bendy is our star, the biggest cartoon character currently in production. Throughout the studio, you might find movie posters or cardboard cutouts of Bendy recycled from various theatrical promotions. Beware when opening closets—some of our more playful employees have rigged Bendy to jump out at you!

Bendy also features in various inspirational posters or workplace reminders. We love our main squeeze, and we think his constant, vigilant watch is a great reminder of the care we put into all the characters at the studio.

Directions:

After turning the pressure valve and flipping the switch on the Power Station, be sure that you've finished everything you need on this level, then visit the Ink Machine Room to turn on the machine. You'll notice some inky footprints leading from the Ink Machine Room into a locked door at the end of the hallway. You will find the Ink Machine Room boarded up, at which point Bendy "will present" himself.

New Objective:
ESCAPE THE WORKSHOP

Survive long enough to make your way back to the entrance, and you will fall through the floor.

New Objective:
DRAIN THE INK

Wade to the valve located in the corner of the room and turn it to drain the ink. Head through the doorway and down the stairs to locate the second valve. Continue downstairs to find the third valve. Once the ink drains, you'll be able to enter through the doorway and locate the axe.

Safety Precautions

Joey Drew Studios is proud to say we have never had a (bad) accident on the job. But due to insurance requirements, we are obligated to stock our studio with the tools you need in the event of a natural disaster, fire, or flood that might require evacuation.

AXE

In various points of location throughout the studio, axes are available to help if you ever need to clear a path to an exit. While some offices have frivolous things like fire extinguishers and first-aid kits, we are proud to offer our employees the best of the best . . . an axe.

IMAGINATION

We pride ourselves on hiring staff of incredible ingenuity. Should an intruder enter the building and demand all of your precious sketches, you might think, *What can I do?* The real question is, *What can't you do?* Creativity can help you out of nearly any situation, and if it can't, well . . . there's always that axe!

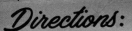

Directions:

Pick up the axe from the table. You can swing it at objects in your path to clear them out of the way.

New Objective:
CLEAR A NEW PATH

Clear the boards from the hallway and in front of the doorway to enter the Ritual Room. Step into the transmutation circle to trigger the next story event, and the end of Chapter 1.

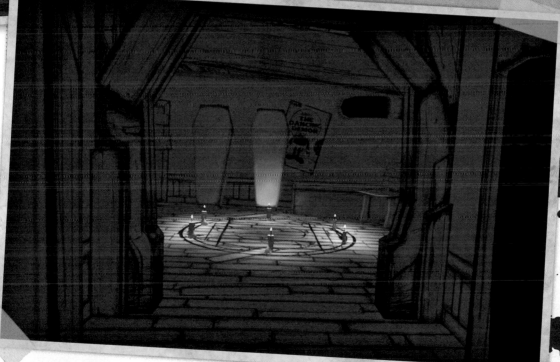

THE CREATOR LIED

CHAPTER TWO
"THE OLD SONG"

Studio Layout

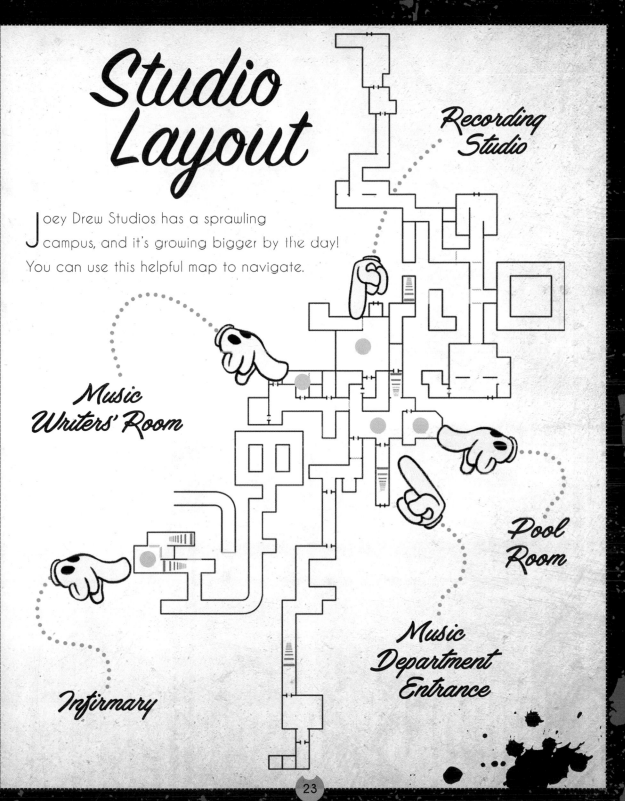

Joey Drew Studios has a sprawling campus, and it's growing bigger by the day! You can use this helpful map to navigate.

Recording Studio

Music Writers' Room

Pool Room

Music Department Entrance

Infirmary

Directions:

After colliding with the transmutation circle, you'll wake up on the floor. Grab the axe and clear the door in front of you. Walking through, you'll come to a large room lit with candles and an audio log from Sammy Lawrence.

Voice of
SAMMY LAWRENCE

He appears from the shadows to rain his sweet blessings upon me. The figure of ink that shines in the darkness. I see you, my savior. I pray you hear me.

Those old songs, I still sing them. For I know you are coming to save me. And I will be swept into your final loving embrace.

But, love requires sacrifice. Can I get an amen?

Directions:

Walking through the flooded hallway, you'll see an inky figure—Sammy Lawrence—carrying a Bendy cutout. He disappears into the wall, but you can still hear him if you approach the wall and listen closely. He says, "Sheep, sheep, it's time for sleep. In the morning, you may wake, or in the morning, you'll be dead."

Continue to the right to find a closed gate that you'll need to power to continue.

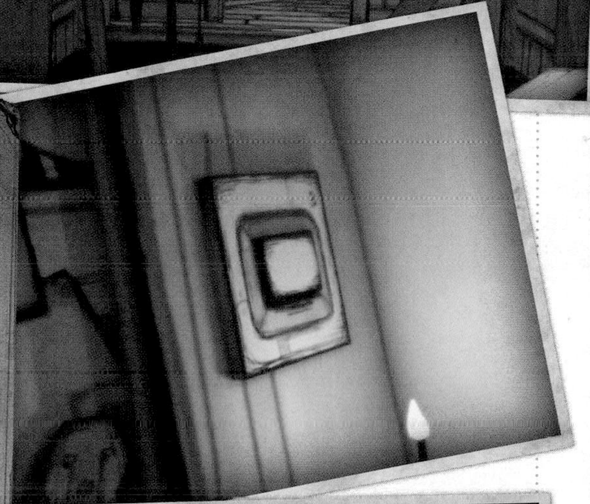

New Objective:

REDIRECT POWER TO THE GATE

You'll find the first switch to the left of the "Bendy in Train Trouble" poster. The second switch is in an alcove to the right of two coffins leaning against a wall. The third switch is at the end of the ink-flooded hallway. You'll need to eat a few cans of Bacon Soup to clear the way to the switch beneath them.

UNDEFEATABLE BENDY

If you use your axe to destroy the Bendy cardboard cutouts that appear over a transmutation circle, you'll find they have reappeared, entirely intact, when you next return to the same spot.

New Objective:

RAISE THE GATE

After raising the gate, clear the doorway to enter the Music Department.

The Music Department

At Joey Drew Studios, it takes all kinds of talent to create a masterpiece, from character artists to animators to voice actors to the very theaters that bring our cartoons to the masses. And a vital part of every cartoon is the music.

Here in the Music Department you'll find our state-of-the-art recording studio. Each month our music director, Sammy Lawrence, brings the best musicians from around the country to our studio to record the music and sound effects that underpin every Joey Drew cartoon. A projector above the recording hall helps the orchestra and voice actors stay in sync and make adjustments to the music as they perform. Mr. Lawrence himself composes each song and oversees its recording to ensure it is expertly produced from start to finish.

JOEY DREW STUDIOS

MUSIC DEPARTMENT

DIRECTOR: SAMMY LAWRENCE

Voice of
SAMMY LAWRENCE

So first, Joey installs this Ink Machine over our heads. Then it begins to leak. Three times last month, we couldn't even get out of our department because the ink had flooded the stairwell.

Joey's solution? An ink pump to drain it periodically. Now I have this ugly pump switch right in my office. People in and out all day.

Thanks, Joey. Just what I needed. More distractions. These stupid cartoon songs don't write themselves, you know.

THE LIGHTER SIDE OF HELL

New Objective:

DRAIN THE STAIRWELL

Entering the Music Department, you'll find that the stairwell to the exit is flooded. You'll need to find a way to drain it. Flip the power switch in the stairwell to turn on the lights.

After returning from the stairwell, you'll be attacked by seven Searchers. These humanoid blobs emerge from ink puddles or leaks in the ink pipes. Two hits with an axe can dispatch a Searcher, or one hit directly to the head. Taking five hits from a Searcher will land you at a respawn point. These enemies may seem like small fries, but if they set upon you in a pack, they can take you down quickly. Try funneling them through a doorway and walking backward as you swing the axe.

Recreation

You've no doubt heard the old adage about "all work and no play." While our company doesn't necessarily condone that philosophy, we can see the value in allowing our employees the chance to blow off steam from time to time. For this reason, various departments are equipped with recreational activities, including darts or billiards. These activities are off-limits to employees and will be locked during work hours, but are available during federally required meal breaks.

Of course, don't expect any kind of reward for obtaining a bull's-eye or sinking a "trick shot" at pool. Time is money, after all.

Directions:
Defeating the Searchers in the Music Department opens a secret pool room to the right of the "Sent from Above" poster. You can play by clicking on the cue ball, which appears to be an eye.

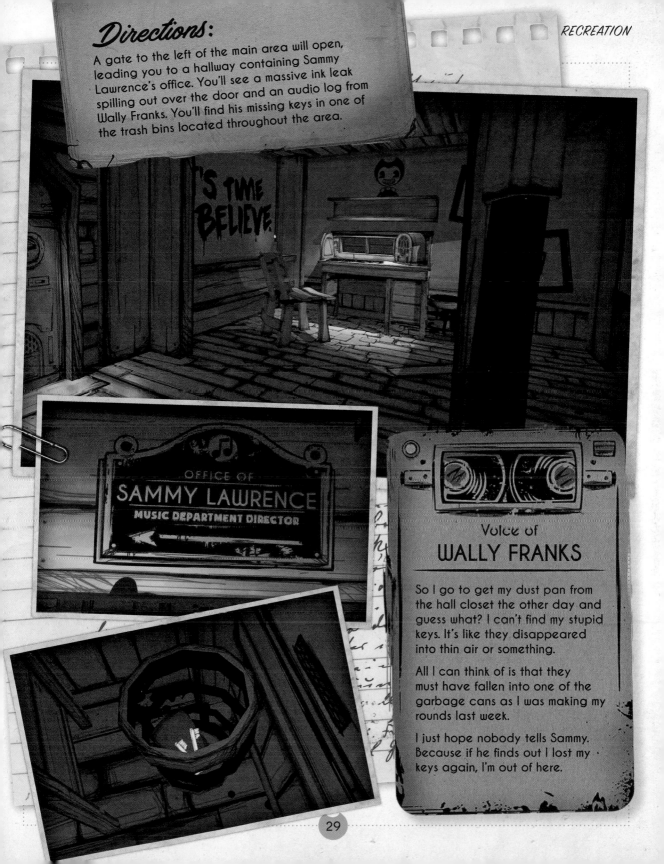

Directions:

A gate to the left of the main area will open, leading you to a hallway containing Sammy Lawrence's office. You'll see a massive ink leak spilling out over the door and an audio log from Wally Franks. You'll find his missing keys in one of the trash bins located throughout the area.

OFFICE OF
SAMMY LAWRENCE
MUSIC DEPARTMENT DIRECTOR

Voice of
WALLY FRANKS

So I go to get my dust pan from the hall closet the other day and guess what? I can't find my stupid keys. It's like they disappeared into thin air or something.

All I can think of is that they must have fallen into one of the garbage cans as I was making my rounds last week.

I just hope nobody tells Sammy. Because if he finds out I lost my keys again, I'm out of here.

Storage Closets

Y ou'll find storage closets throughout Joey Drew Studios. These closets are generally owned by different departments and are often used for supplies. If you belong to a department that has access to a closet, you can ask your manager for keys to it; otherwise most closets usually remain locked to deter thieves or inefficiency.

Some closets belong to the maintenance staff, headed by the aforementioned Wally Franks. Mr. Franks does his best to keep our sprawling studio sparkling clean with the supplies he's budgeted, so please refrain from taking any items from his janitorial closets.

Directions:
Taking the keys back to the right of Sammy's office, you'll find a door labeled "Closet" that will now be unlocked. Inside is another audio log and a new objective.

New Objective:
FIND SAMMY'S SANCTUARY

Voice of
SAMMY LAWRENCE

Every artistic person needs a sanctuary. Joey Drew has his and I have mine. To enter, you need only know my favorite song.

Directions:

Before completing this section, you may want to check out the "Strike Up the Band" achievement on page 39. Note that Sammy's favorite song changes with each game, so you will likely have a different instrument or instrument order.

Return to the area you first entered, and walk up the stairs to the right. You'll find an audio log from Norman Polk as well as a projector you can turn on. Activate the projector, then go downstairs to the recording studio. Interact with the instruments in Sammy's song in the correct order to open his sanctuary.

New Objective:
ENTER THE SANCTUARY

Voice of
NORMAN POLK

Every day, the same strange thing happens. I'll be up here in my booth, the band will be swinging, and suddenly Sammy Lawrence just comes marching in and shuts the whole thing down. Tells us all to wait in the hall.

Then I hear him. He starts up my projector, and he dashes from the projector booth and down to the recording studio like the little devil himself was chasing behind.

Few seconds later, the projector turns off. But Sammy, he doesn't come out for a long time. This man is weird. Crazy weird.

I have half a mind to talk to Mister Drew about all this. But then again, I have to admit, Mister Drew has his own peculiarities.

SING A HAPPY SONG. WHISTLE A MERRY TUNE. WAIT FOR HIS ARRIVAL, HE'S COMING VERY SOON.

Directions:

The gate to the left of the recording booth will rise, granting you access to Sammy's sanctuary. Inside you'll find a valve to adjust the ink pressure. Turn the valve and proceed back out to the recording studio. You'll catch a glimpse of Sammy himself, watching you, from a balcony to the left of the projector booth.

As he watches, seven Searchers will attack you on your way to the door. If possible, try herding them in a row as you back into Sammy's sanctuary, so as not to become overwhelmed.

From: Joey Drew

Memo to Staff Regarding New Initiatives

I'm excited to reveal that Joey Drew Studios will be embarking on a new initiative that's sure to take our studio straight to the top!

All staff and talent are asked to gather in the main lobby at 4:30 PM this Friday to meet Alice Angel, the newest friend of Bendy and Boris the Wolf. Refreshments will be served, along with the chance to meet the voice of Alice herself, Susie Campbell. Don't be late!

Alice Angel

Voice of
SUSIE CAMPBELL

It may only be my second month working for Joey Drew, but I can already tell I'm going to love it here!

People really seem to enjoy my Alice Angel voice. Sammy says she may be as popular as Bendy someday.

These past few weeks I have voiced everything, from talking chairs to dancing chickens. But this is the first character I have really felt a connection with. Like she's part of me.

Alice and I, we are going places.

Medical Needs

FEELING SICK?
WOKE UP WITH AN ACHING BACK?
SLIPPED ON A PUDDLE OF INK?

There's no need to recuperate at home—come visit the Infirmary! Our friendly medical staff is on call several hours each week to tend to your needs. Full-time staff members with **GENUINE ILLNESS OR INJURY** are encouraged to check in at the Infirmary for rest and care. The Infirmary's trained staff will have you up, running, and back to your desk in no time, to ensure your work remains in tip-top shape! If you find that staff is unavailable at the time of your visit, feel free to help yourself to our assortment of first-aid supplies before returning to your desk to finish out the workday.

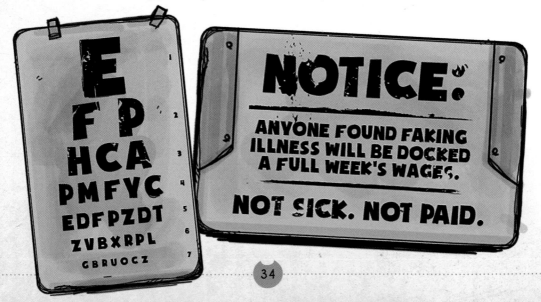

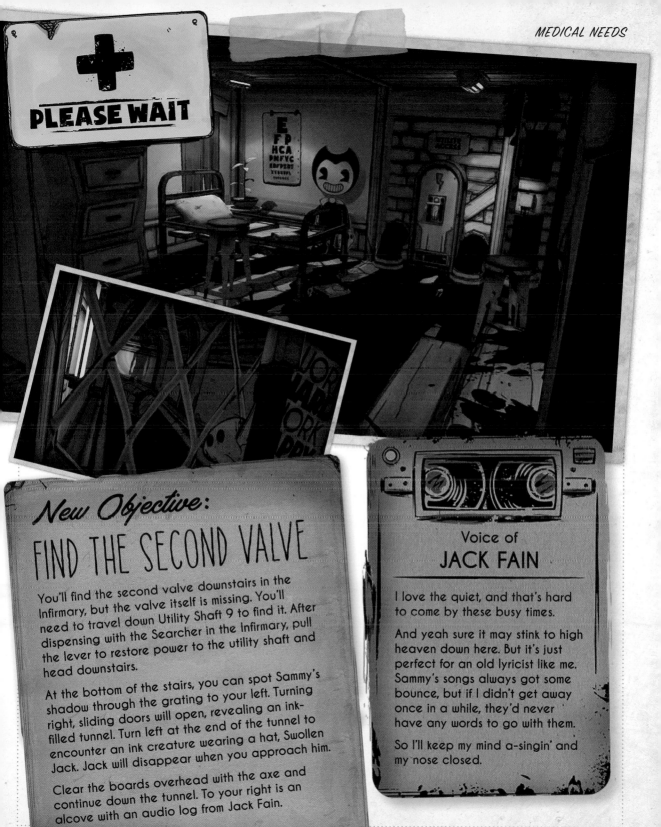

PLEASE WAIT

E
F P
H C A
D N F V C

New Objective:
FIND THE SECOND VALVE

You'll find the second valve downstairs in the Infirmary, but the valve itself is missing. You'll need to travel down Utility Shaft 9 to find it. After dispensing with the Searcher in the Infirmary, pull the lever to restore power to the utility shaft and head downstairs.

At the bottom of the stairs, you can spot Sammy's shadow through the grating to your left. Turning right, sliding doors will open, revealing an ink-filled tunnel. Turn left at the end of the tunnel to encounter an ink creature wearing a hat, Swollen Jack. Jack will disappear when you approach him.

Clear the boards overhead with the axe and continue down the tunnel. To your right is an alcove with an audio log from Jack Fain.

Voice of
JACK FAIN

I love the quiet, and that's hard to come by these busy times.

And yeah sure it may stink to high heaven down here. But it's just perfect for an old lyricist like me. Sammy's songs always got some bounce, but if I didn't get away once in a while, they'd never have any words to go with them.

So I'll keep my mind a-singin' and my nose closed.

From: Thomas Connor

Memo to Staff Regarding Utility Shafts

To All Concerned.

We know that the noise from the Ink Machine and the new plumbing has made it hard for you all to get your work done, but just a quick reminder that the utility shafts scattered throughout the building are off-limits. It's really not safe for folks to be down there. If a pipe burst, well—you could find yourself in a sticky spot real fast. We've taken the liberty of boarding off some of them for your own protection. Just stay out of there, okay?

SING WITH ME

New Objective:

SWOLLEN JACK

Follow the tunnel until you come to an open boiler room, with Swollen Jack in the back, holding the valve you need. Jack won't attack you and will likely disappear before you can attack him. Even if you do manage a hit, he won't take damage; you will need to outsmart him to obtain the valve. The lever to your left will raise a platform containing a box, while the lever on your right will drop it suddenly. Corral Swollen Jack underneath the platform, then pull the lever to the right to squash him. He'll drop your valve in the process.

Once you grab the valve, return to the Infirmary to restore it to the pipe and close the valve. On the way, you'll notice Sammy's shadow is no longer visible from behind the grating.

New Objective:

RETURN TO SAMMY'S OFFICE

OVERACHIEVER!

A few achievements will be given to you through the natural course of the story:

MY FAVORITE SONG: Solve the music puzzle to open the way to Sammy's sanctuary.

A SPECIAL HAT: Run into Jack Fain.

THE BELIEVER: Survive being chased by Bendy.

But before you head to Sammy's office to finish *Chapter 2: "The Old Song,"* be sure to check the following items off your to-do list:

COAST TO COAST: Turn on the radio, which you'll find in Sammy's office.

JOHNNY'S BROKEN HEART: Head down the hallway that leads to Sammy's office. The first door on your right opens into a room with a pipe organ. Play the organ five times, waiting after each time to hear a moaning voice, and you will unlock this achievement.

STRIKE UP THE BAND: For this achievement, you'll need to travel from the booth to the stage. Repeat this ten times, noting that a new Bendy cutout appears onstage with each trip (up to nine Bendys in all). When you successfully open the sanctuary, all the Bendys will appear up in the loft where you saw Sammy lurking.

MAN BEHIND THE CURTAIN: Visit theMeatly. Go down the hallway toward Sammy's office and enter the second door on the right. Walk through the "Sheep Songs" poster to the right of the first desk.

OLD PROBLEMS: Listen to all the audio logs in this chapter. There are seven:

- Three from Sammy Lawrence: One before the ink-flooded hallway, one when you enter the Music Department, and one in the supply closet.
- One from Wally Franks outside Sammy's office.
- One from Susie Campbell by the piano in the recording studio.
- One from Norman Polk in the projector booth above the recording studio.
- One from Jack Fain in Utility Shaft 9.

CANADIAN BACON: Collect all the Bacon Soup in this chapter (see page 40).

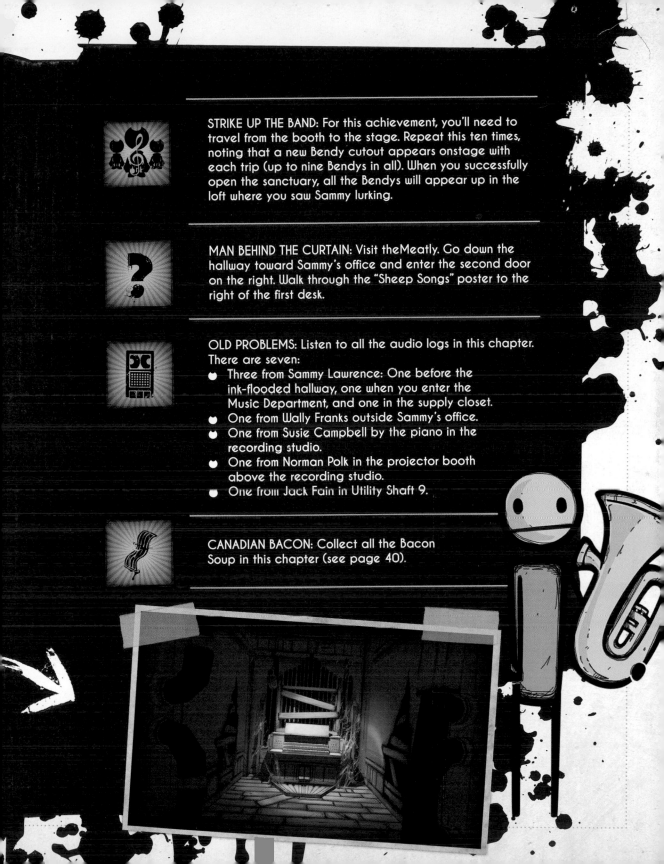

STUDIO LAYOUT

BRIAR LABEL
BACON SOUP

CANADIAN BACON

There are thirty-one cans of Bacon Soup scattered throughout the studio in Chapter 2. Be sure to get them all for the "Canadian Bacon" achievement.

- Three cans, in the shelving underneath the "He will set us free" writing on the wall.
- Twenty cans, in the shelves near the third switch.
- One can, on the first desk you see when you walk into the office.
- Four cans, in the supply closet outside of Sammy's office.
- One can, on Jack Fain's piano down Utility Shaft 9.

After Sammy knocks you out . . .

- One can, when you're free from Sammy, walk straight, in front of the loose boards, then to the right. You'll find a Bendy statue, and one can to the right of its feet, beside a barrel.
- One can, after escaping Bendy, on top of a barrel in front of a shelf of Bendy toys.

Briar Label Bacon Soup

By now, we're sure you're wondering, *What's with all the soup?*

As part of Bendy's licensing agreement with Briar Label Bacon Soup, the Briar Label Company has stocked Joey Drew Studios from roof to sub-sub-sub-sub-basement with free soup as a thank-you. Made from a traditional family recipe, Briar Label Bacon Soup tastes just like the home-kitchen cooking that Mom used to make. Rather than going out for lunch, please indulge in a free meal on us while you work at your desk—forks are available upon request.

After eating, please leave your dirty bowls in the dedicated shelving in the stairwell for Wally Franks. And don't forget to rinse and deposit your tin cans in salvage bins to help the war effort!

JUST THE WAY THE LITTLE DEVIL LIKES IT.

New Objective:

THE MINER SEARCHER

Backtrack to the Ritual Room with the transmutation circle (where you started Chapter 2) to unlock a secret boss. You'll need to battle several new Searchers as you backtrack. From the transmutation circle, a new boss forms—an ink creature wearing a hard hat. This Miner Searcher does a significant amount of damage if it hits you, so be careful. You can do several things with this creature:

- You can kill this boss with four swings of your axe, but doing so will result in nothing.

- Lead it back to the boiler room where you squashed Swollen Jack. Squash this creature in the same manner to trigger a creepy noise and a glitching screen. You'll hear the rumbling noise repeat throughout the level. This action is required to obtain the Scythe (see page 142).

JOEY DREW STUDIOS

From: Sammy Lawrence

To: All Staff Regarding the Music Department

Musical instruments aren't just for fun. We do serious work here at the Music Department. While I know it may be tempting, please refrain from playing musical instruments in our corridors.

Just last week I had to rerecord a song because someone was plucking a banjo just outside the recording studio. Whoever it was, please stop it. And please, everyone, stop making so much noise in general. No more loud shoes, whistling, humming, or gum chewing by the Music Department.

You have been warned.

"THERE WE GO NOW. NICE AND TIGHT. WE WOULDN'T WANT OUR SHEEP ROAMING AWAY NOW, WOULD WE? NO, WE WOULDN'T. I MUST ADMIT I AM HONORED YOU CAME ALL THE WAY DOWN HERE TO VISIT ME. IT ALMOST MAKES WHAT I'M ABOUT TO DO SEEM CRUEL. BUT THE BELIEVERS MUST HONOR THEIR SAVIOR. I MUST HAVE HIM NOTICE ME. WAIT. YOU LOOK FAMILIAR TO ME . . . THAT FACE . . . NOT NOW. FOR OUR LORD IS CALLING TO US, MY LITTLE SHEEP. THE TIME OF SACRIFICE IS AT HAND! AND THEN, I WILL FINALLY BE FREED FROM THIS PRISON. THIS INKY, DARK ABYSS I CALL A BODY. SHHHH. QUIET! LISTEN! I CAN HEAR HIM. CRAWLING ABOVE. CRAWLING! LET US BEGIN. THE RITUAL MUST BE COMPLETED! SOON HE WILL HEAR ME . . . HE WILL SET US FREE."

Directions:

Sammy then leaves the room to summon Ink Bendy. As you struggle to get free, you can hear Ink Bendy turn on Sammy, attacking him. A pool of ink will leak out from under the door Sammy went through, and you're able to free yourself.

New Objective:
ESCAPE BENDY

Dispatch the five Searchers in the room and head through the newly opened gate. Break the boards in the hallway to clear a path. In the first alcove to your right, you'll be able to get a peek at the Ink Machine lowering from the upper level. After chopping up the last board in the hallway, your axe will break.

Ink Bendy will appear in the ink-flooded room at the end of the hall, and you'll have to escape him. More and more ink will pool on the walls and floor as Ink Bendy gets closer, so be sure to stay ahead of him. Eventually you'll get to a room and the door will lock behind you. Continue on to encounter Boris the Wolf.

After your axe breaks, linger in the hallway for a minute just outside the ink-flooded room where Ink Bendy appears. If you stay for long enough, you'll be able to hear Bendy's whistle, which you also heard in the Theater in Chapter 1.

CHAPTER THREE
"RISE AND FALL"

New Objective:
LEAVE THE SAFEHOUSE

Studio Layout

Joey Drew Studios has a sprawling campus, and it's growing bigger by the day! You can use this helpful map to navigate.

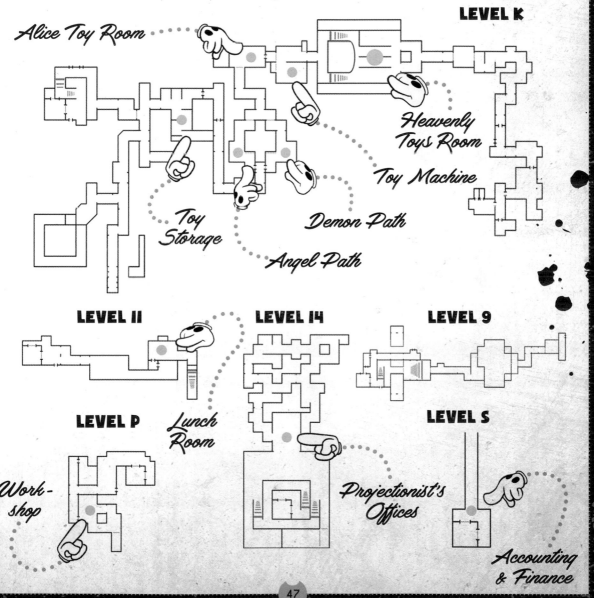

LEVEL K

Alice Toy Room

Heavenly Toys Room

Toy Machine

Toy Storage

Demon Path

Angel Path

LEVEL 11

LEVEL 14

LEVEL 9

LEVEL P

Lunch Room

LEVEL S

Work-shop

Projectionist's Offices

Accounting & Finance

Boris the Wolf

Every animated character needs a best pal, and Bendy has one in Boris the Wolf! Boris isn't quite as bright as Bendy, so he often ends up with the short end of the stick in Bendy's schemes. Through it all, Boris stays loyal to his friends, so long as they don't come between him and his lunch!

From Joey Drew

When we first had the idea for Bendy, we were so excited, but our little devil got bored quickly. What's the point of a laugh if you can't share it with your pals? We created Boris the Wolf mainly to keep things interesting, but he quickly evolved into one of our company's favorite characters. I mean, can you imagine the joy of wearing overalls every day? Our animators should know, though, that there's a lot more to Boris than meets the eye. Is he perhaps a wolf in sheep's clothing after all? Maybe you'll tell us!

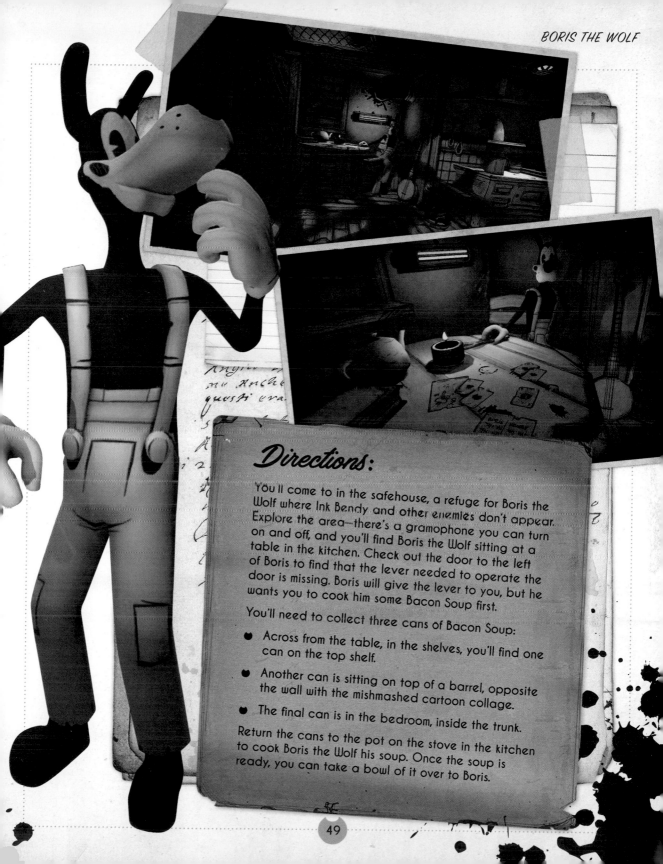

Directions:

You'll come to in the safehouse, a refuge for Boris the Wolf where Ink Bendy and other enemies don't appear. Explore the area—there's a gramophone you can turn on and off, and you'll find Boris the Wolf sitting at a table in the kitchen. Check out the door to the left of Boris to find that the lever needed to operate the door is missing. Boris will give the lever to you, but he wants you to cook him some Bacon Soup first.

You'll need to collect three cans of Bacon Soup:

- ❤ Across from the table, in the shelves, you'll find one can on the top shelf.

- ❤ Another can is sitting on top of a barrel, opposite the wall with the mishmashed cartoon collage.

- ❤ The final can is in the bedroom, inside the trunk.

Return the cans to the pot on the stove in the kitchen to cook Boris the Wolf his soup. Once the soup is ready, you can take a bowl of it over to Boris.

New Objective:
FIND THE EXIT

As soon as Boris is satisfied, he'll take out a box containing the lever you'll need. Place the lever handle on the mechanism to the left of the door and pull it to open. Boris will hop up from the table to leave. You won't be able to return to the safehouse once you exit it, so proceed with caution.

New Objective:
ENTER THE DARKNESS

Wander ahead with Boris until you come to a long, dark hallway. You'll need to retrieve the flashlight from a desk to the right before entering the darkness.

In the dark corridor, you'll see moving gears, ink jars, and splattering ink. Boris will get scared and stop moving, so keep the light near him! Continue on until you reach a room that appears to be a dead end, where it's a little brighter. Once you reach this room, the door will close behind you.

From here, you'll need to give Boris your flashlight so he can crawl through the vents to open the door. After a minute or so, the doors will slide open, clearing your way toward the Heavenly Toys Room.

GIVE A WOLF A BONE
Before you leave the safehouse, check out this fun Easter egg: return to the bedroom, where you'll find a bone to the left of the trunk. You can give it to Boris, who will gnaw on it throughout the chapter. This will also earn you the "Knick-Knack Paddywhack" achievement.

New Objective:
FIND THE EXIT

JOEY DREW STUDIOS UNVEILS TOYS

New York, NY—Joey Drew Studios has recently unveiled their new toy line, featuring characters from the innovative animation studio. The toys will be produced within the studio under the new subsidiary Heavenly Toys.

"We are thrilled to bring Bendy, Boris the Wolf, and many other beloved characters to toy form," said Joey Drew, president and founder of the company. "It is our biggest dream that, one day, Bendy and his friends will be part of every child in America's day to day."

The runaway success of the little cartoon devil, Bendy, continues to take America by storm. The company

even has further plans to expand into apparel, publishing, and toothpaste.

"To encourage dreams and—almost equally important—proper oral hygiene," added Drew.

Heavenly Toys' first products will debut on shelves later this year, just in time for the holidays. The little devil is sure to have parents and children alike lining up outside the toy store bright and early to get a new plush Bendy friend of their own!

New Objective:
FIX THE TOY MACHINE

As you head into the Heavenly Toys Room, you can faintly hear someone humming. Head up the steps and into the workshop. The toy machine in the workshop is broken, and you'll need to fix it if you want to clear a path to access the rooms beyond.

Go back into the Heavenly Toys Room and find the lever by the staircase. Once there, pull it. Next you'll need to unclog the belt wheels by collecting the toys that are stuck in them. You'll need to collect four plush toys before continuing on.

INK BLOB

If you're planning to complete the "Blazing Metal" achievement, squeeze into the little alcove where Shawn Flynn's audio log is. Interact with the ink blob on the desk until it takes the shape of a tiny Ink Machine. If you're interested in the Lever Challenge, morph the ink blob into Boris.

Voice of
SHAWN FLYNN

I don't be seein' what the big deal is.

So what if I went and painted some of those Bendy dolls with a crooked smile?

That's sure no reason for Mister Drew to be flyin' off the handle at me. And if he really wants to be so helpful, he could be tellin' me what I'm to be doin' with this warehouse I got full of that angel whatchamacallit. Not a scrap of that mess be a-sellin'! Probably have to melt it all down to be rid of it all.

New Objective:
TURN ON THE TOY MACHINE

Now you'll need to turn the machine on. On the right side of the room, pull the lever that's located between two of the belt wheels. Several shelves of toys will slide away, revealing an unlocked door.

THE ERIE D

LATE CIT

12 September 1933

JOEY DR DEBUTS

New York, NY—Joining the ranks of beloved cartoon characters Bendy and Boris the Wolf is Alice Angel, the newest character at Joey Drew Studios.

"It has always been part of our plan to bring a dynamic, strong, and intelligent character like Alice to the table," said Joey Drew, president and founder of the company. "Alice isn't your typical girl next door. She's a character with charm, but brains too. When Bendy is getting up to something, Alice is there to throw a wrench into his schemes."

As the first female character for Joey Drew Studios, Alice Angel certainly

AILY TIMES

EDITION   TWO CENTS

EW STUDIOS ALICE ANGEL

has a lot to live up to. We asked Joey what kind of gal Alice Angel will be.

"What kind of gal? Well, she's quite a gal," said Joey Drew with a wry smile. "She sings; she dances. We think Alice's fiery, sharp character will really resonate with Bendy fans, and we're excited to introduce her to our animation cartoons and merchandise."

Alice Angel merchandise will be available next year through Joey Drew Studios' upcoming toy line, Heavenly Toys. She will be voiced by actress Susie Campbell.

ALICE ANGEL'S CHAMBER

Through the unblocked door you will enter a new room—Alice Angel's chamber. The lights will go out, and several TV screens will flicker to life, singing Alice's theme song. Through the glass window straight ahead, you'll meet the twisted Alice Angel for the first time. She will scream, break the glass, and escape into the room.

SHE'S QUITE A GAL!

Voice of
JOEY DREW

There's nothing wrong with dreaming. Wishing for the impossible is just human nature. That's how I got started. Just a pencil and a dream. We all want everything without even having to lift a finger.

They say you just have to believe.

Belief can make you succeed. Belief can make you rich. Belief can make you powerful.

Why, with enough belief, you can even cheat death itself.

Now that . . . is a beautiful, and positively silly thought.

ALICE ANGEL

I'm the cutest little angel, sent from above, and I know just how to swing.

I got a bright little halo, and I'm filled with love . . .

I'm Alice Angel!

I'm the hit of the party, I'm the belle of the ball, I'm the toast of every town.

Just one little dance, and I know you'll fall . . .

I'm Alice Angel!

I ain't no flapper, I'm a classy dish, and boy, can this girl sing.

This gal can grant your every wish . . .

I'm Alice Angel!

New Objective:
FIND A NEW EXIT

When the lights come back on, turn to your left to walk through several narrow corridors until you come to a fork in the path and a sign. You can choose one of two routes: The "Demon" route, and the "Angel" route. Taking each path is an achievement, but if you're looking to accomplish the "Blazing Metal" achievement, you'll need to take the Demon path. Take the Angel path if you'd like to complete the Lever Challenge.

THE ANGEL
Choose the right side and you'll find a brightly lit room with a couch and an audio recording from Susie Campbell.

THE DEMON
THE DEMON
Veer to the left and you'll walk through the Demon route, which is flooded with ink. Here you will encounter a new audio recording from Joey Drew.

Voice of
SUSIE CAMPBELL

Everything feels like it's coming apart.

When I walked into the recording booth today, Sammy was there with that . . . Allison.

Apparently, I didn't get the memo. Alice Angel will now be voiced by Miss Allison Pendle.

A part of me died when he said that.

There's gotta be a way to fix this!

From: Joey Drew

To: All Staff

Please give a warm welcome to Allison Pendle, Joey Drew Studios' newest employee. Allison is a talented voice actress with lots of dreams. In her spare time, she loves to cook and invent recipes. I know that as soon as you meet her, you'll be taken with her beautiful voice and charm. She's so interesting, so . . . different. I have to say, I'm an instant fan.

Effective immediately, Allison will be the new voice of Alice Angel. We believe this restructure in voice talent will lead to a more cohesive character list—and more success for our dreams.

Allison will meet with Sammy Lawrence after lunch to discuss rerecording Alice Angel's dialogue. Then I will bring her around to meet everyone.

Distribute immediately to all employees except for Susie Campbell.

Directions:
Press on, and you'll get a Bendy cutout jump scare, courtesy of Boris. Boris has returned with a Gent pipe you can use to arm yourself.

New Objective:
ARM YOURSELF

Through the door you'll find an ink-flooded room with toys, clocks, and stuffed animals based on the studio's animated characters. Boris will lead you to a Bendy statue; here, you'll find the first of two switches.

BENDY IN

15 5 CEN

"THE BUTCHER GANG!

PRESENTED IN SILLYVISION

New Objective:
OPEN THE STORAGE EXIT

Turn around and follow the cables to the second switch, which appears to the left of a poster for the Butcher Gang. The poster will break open to reveal a Piper, the twisted version of cartoon Charley from the Butcher Gang. You will need to hit this enemy roughly six times in order to defeat him. Only then will the lever become available to you.

Before flipping the lever, explore the area. Coming back toward Boris, the first corridor on the left will lead you to several discoveries. There's an audio log from Wally Franks and Thomas Connor sitting in the hallway. The first room on the right will give you a view of the Ink Machine being lowered once again.

New Objective:
FIND A NEW EXIT

After you're done exploring, return and flip the lever, following Boris through to the new exit. You'll come out into an open area with a marking for Level K and a large elevator.

Upon entering the elevator, you and Boris will hear Alice Angel's voice as you descend lower and lower. The elevator will bring you to Level 9 of the studio, where Alice resides.

Voice of
WALLY and THOMAS

Wally: Alright, let's go over this again. If the pressure goes over 45, I screw the safety bolt in tighter, right?

Thomas: No! For the last time, you do that, you'll blow every pipe in this place! If it reaches 45, you unhook the safety switch.

Wally: You sure? You know, this sounds harder than comparing ear wax to bee's wax!

Thomas: Look, it's not that difficult! Just keep an eye on the gauge!

Wally: Look pal, if you think I'm doing my job AND yours, I'm outta here!

Voice of
THOMAS CONNOR

These blasted elevators . . . sometimes they open, sometimes they don't . . . sometimes they come . . . sometimes they keep on going to hell and back.

I keep telling these people, if Mister Joey Drew keeps cutting corners like this, someone's sure to end up falling to their death. And it sure ain't gonna be me.

I'm taking the stairs.

New Objective:
DATE WITH AN ANGEL

Exit the elevator and head down a flight of stairs to encounter an audio log from Thomas Connor.

Directions:

Descend the set of stairs in front of you, then head across the bridge to another flight of stairs, this time leading up to a closed doorway with Alice Angel's face and slogan atop it. As you near it with Boris, the doors will slide open. Boris will run through the narrow hallway and you will follow him, passing a cardboard cutout of Alice as you go.

In the new room, you'll find multiple clones of Boris and Charley, each one sacrificed to make Alice beautiful and more "perfect." As you explore the room, you'll find an audio log from Susie Campbell.

Continue on through the corridors until you come upon twisted Alice, who will tell you about how she became an "angel," as she describes it. Alice says she will let you leave if you perform various errands for her.

"DO YOU KNOW WHAT IT'S LIKE? LIVING IN THE DARK PUDDLES? IT'S A BUZZING, SCREAMING WELL OF VOICES! BITS OF YOUR MIND, SWIMMING... LIKE... FISH IN A BOWL! THE FIRST TIME I WAS BORN FROM ITS INKY WOMB, I WAS A WIGGLING, PUSSING, SHAPELESS SLUG. THE SECOND TIME... WELL... IT MADE ME AN ANGEL! I WILL NOT LET THE DEMON TOUCH ME AGAIN. I'M SO CLOSE NOW. SO... ALMOST PERFECT."

New Objective:
DO THE ANGEL'S BIDDING

Voice of
SUSIE CAMPBELL

Who would have thought? Me having lunch with Joey Drew! Apparently times are tougher than I thought.

For a moment there, I thought I'd be stuck with the check. But I gotta say, he wasn't at all what I expected. Quite the charmer. He even called me Alice. I liked it!

Joe's Fine Dining

555 Christopher Street, New York, NY

For the finest quality at reasonable prices, Joe's Fine Dining cannot be beat!

NO REFUNDS ACCEPTED

2	Bacon Soup
1	Linguini Alfredo
1	Filet Mignon
1	Iced Tea
1	Lemonade
1	Strawberry Cheesecake

Joe's Fine Dining

555 Christopher Street, New York, NY

For the finest quality at reasonable prices, Joe's Fine Dining cannot be beat!

NO REFUNDS ACCEPTED

2	Bacon Soup
1	Linguini Alfredo
1	Filet Mignon
1	Iced Tea
1	Lemonade
1	Strawberry Cheesecake

Welcome lunch for Susie Campbell. Quite the charmer.

New Objective: COLLECT THREE GEARS

New Objective: TAKE THE WRENCH

After returning to the elevator, trade your Gent pipe for a wrench, which you can collect from the revolving cupboard to the left of the "She's quite a gal!" sliding doors. Enter the elevator and travel back to Level K to collect three gears for Alice's machines. From the elevator, take the stairs up and head through the corridor.

1. You'll likely find the first gear in the hands of a Piper, the twisted version of Charley from the Butcher Gang. Defeat him to obtain it.

2. As you backtrack into the storage area, you'll see maintenance panels on the walls, which will contain the remaining gears. Many of these panels are empty, but the second gear can be found by opening the panel on the left side of the storage room, between the two shelves of toys.

3. The final gear can be found at the end of the long hallway on the right side of the storage room. You will have to defeat a Searcher to access it.

New Objective: RETURN TO THE ANGEL

Return to Alice on Level 9, and deposit the gears into the drop box to the right of the sliding doors.

New Objective: TAKE THE INK SYRINGE

INK BENDY

Throughout this chapter, you may be set upon by Ink Bendy. You'll be able to see him approach by the weblike lines of ink that appear over the floor and grow darker the closer Ink Bendy gets. When you see him approach, make your way to a Little Miracle Station and get inside. Ink Bendy cannot attack you in here; wait until the lines of ink disappear before exiting.

New Objective:
COLLECT THREE EXTRA THICK INK

Take the Ink Syringe Alice will provide you and head up to Level 11, and walk straight out of the elevators down the hallway, fighting the Searchers along the way.

1. Fight the Fisher, the corrupted version of Barley from the Butcher Gang, wandering around the level. After defeating him, a pulsing glob of ink will appear on the ground, which you can collect.

2. Continue straight back into an open room with a stream of ink flowing toward a Little Miracle Station. Outside the station, a Swollen Searcher will form. Defeat it to obtain your second glob of ink.

3. In the corner opposite where you found the first Swollen Searcher, another will form. This Searcher will sometimes disappear and reappear in the back of the room. Defeat it to get the final glob of ink.

In the back of the room with the two Swollen Searchers is a room with a window. Here you'll get your first peek at the Projectionist, whom you'll encounter later in this chapter. An audio log from Wally Franks also appears here.

Voice of
WALLY FRANKS

I don't get it.

Everyone's walking around here like grandma just died. Nothing but angry faces everywhere.

These people gotta lighten up. I mean hello! You make cartoons! Your job is to make people laugh.

I'm tellin' ya, if these people don't start crackin' a smile every now and then, I'm outta here.

New Objective:
RETURN TO THE ANGEL

BEFORE YOU RETURN TO ALICE... Head into the stairway on Level 11 to find an alcove full of musical instruments. Play the bass, drum, violin, piano, and drum in that order to hear a secret message from Sammy Lawrence.

"WE'VE ALL BEEN WAITING, BUT NOW, HE WILL SET... US... FREE..."

Directions:

As before, deposit the extra thick ink into the drop box. Your syringe will disappear and you'll be given a plunger.

New Objective:
TAKE THE PLUNGER

New Objective:
COLLECT THREE VALVE CORES

Take the elevator or stairs to Level P. From the elevator, make a U-turn down a hallway into a large open room. Straight ahead you'll see three glass walls encasing another room.

1. The first valve core is obtained from defeating a Striker, the demented version of Edgar from the Butcher Gang, which should wander up to you.

2. Enter the glass room on the right, which you'll see when walking away from the elevator. Here you'll find three valves below three tubes of ink set into the nonglass wall. Each tube has a dot in the middle. Turn the valves until all the ink levels match the dots. When they do, a door to the left of the valves will open, containing the second valve core.

3. Exit the first glass room and continue straight down the hallway to enter another glass room. Turn right at the "Little Devil Darlin'" poster and make a left, toward a "Hell in a Handbasket" poster. You'll see another set of valves to the right of the poster. Solve this puzzle in the same way to obtain your third valve core.

New Objective:
RETURN TO THE ANGEL

CORPORATION WARRANTY

A SPECIAL PROMISE TO OUR CUSTOMERS

At Gent Corporation, we strive to make the best products possible for our customers. With quality craftsmanship, friendly staff, and expert machinists, we're certain you'll be satisfied with our products and service. If you follow our service manual to the letter and suffer a malfunction with your Gent device, we will be happy to send one of our qualified staff members to assist you, for as long as it takes to make things right.

This warranty is valid for ten years of service, no matter the issue, big or small!

WARRANTY

New Objective:
TAKE THE AXE

Directions:

Back on Level 9, leave the valve cores in the drop box to obtain your new tool, the axe.

New Objective:
DESTROY ALL BENDY CUTOUTS

Return to Level K, where you'll need to destroy all the Bendy cutouts on this level—sixteen in all. To ensure you get all of them, it's easiest to backtrack to the beginning of the level and start there:

- Facing the staircases, there are four Bendy cutouts on the left side of the room.

- There are another four on the right side of the room.

- Heading through Alice Angel's chamber, you'll find one on the path toward the Angel/Demon fork in the path, leaning against a barrel.

- One on the Demon or Angel path (whichever path you took, you'll find one in that room).

- Upon exiting the Demon or Angel path, there's a cutout immediately to your right, leaning against a wall.

- After a series of corridors, you'll find one right outside the door to the storage room.

- There are three in the toy storage room.

- Heading down the stairs toward the elevator, jump over the railing near the landing to destroy the last Bendy cutout to the right of the elevator.

Voice of
GRANT COHEN

They say the real problem with Mister Drew is that he never actually tells us little people anything.

Oh sure, according to him there's always big stuff coming, adventure and fame and the like.

But I'm the guy, see, who has to make sure our budgets don't go all out of whack just 'cause genius upstairs went out and got himself another idea. Speaking of which, and this is top secret, apparently Mister Drew has another large project in mind now . . . and it ain't cheap.

BEFORE YOU RETURN THAT AXE . . .

Before you return to Alice on Level 9, exit the elevators on that level and turn to the left to find a boarded-up door under the "Level 9" sign. Hack away the boards and enter the office to find a secret audio log from Joey Drew Studios' Accounting & Finance Department director, Grant Cohen. There is also a spare axe here, hidden between two crates. Do not pick the axe up; wait until after you return Alice's axe to retrieve this one.

New Objective:
RETURN TO THE ANGEL

Directions:

When you return to Alice, she'll have another task for you: Kill the Butcher Gang.

New Objective:
THE ANGEL'S WRATH

You'll be set upon by several Searchers as well as a Striker, Fisher, and Piper. Dispatching all the enemies will complete your objective.

From here, Alice will send you on one final errand: Say hello to an old friend on a lower level.

– ARM YOURSELF! –

- **GENT PIPE:** If you took none of the special steps below, you will likely face this next challenge with the Gent pipe. Not a terrible weapon, but definitely the least effective for the upcoming task.

- **TOMMY GUN:** If you morphed the ink blob into a tiny Ink Machine back in the Heavenly Toys workshop, took the path of the Demon, and accomplished all of Alice's tasks up to this point without dying, you'll be rewarded with the Tommy gun. This weapon dispatches enemies much faster than the Gent pipe, and at a distance too! The gun will reload after about twenty shots, but ammo is unlimited. Interestingly, Alice says it belonged to someone "very special."

- **GRANT'S SECRET AXE:** Retrieve the secret axe from the boarded-up office on Level 9 (see page 69).

New Objective:
TAKE THE TOMMY GUN

— LEVER CHALLENGE —

If you morphed the ink blob in the Heavenly Toys workshop into Boris, took the path of the Angel, and unblocked the secret office with Grant Cohen's audio log, a special challenge will unlock for you. After dispatching the Butcher Gang and retrieving the secret axe, return to the Toy Workshop. You'll see a wall that's been boarded up from floor to ceiling, to the left of a "Work Hard, Work Happy" sign. Hack away the boards to reveal three levers, labeled "For service, please pull lever."

- Pulling the first lever summons a horde of Searchers.

- Pulling the second lever summons multiple Butcher Gangs.

- Pulling the third lever summons a giant Searcher Boss.

OVERACHIEVER!

A few achievements will be given to you through the natural course of the story:

 DARKER PLACES: Survive the Inky Abyss (where the Projectionist lurks).

 FRONT LINES: Survive the Butcher Gang's attack.

 THE PATH OF THE DEMON: Choose the way of Bendy.

 ANGER MANAGEMENT: Destroy all Bendy cutouts in Chapter 3.

 THE PATH OF THE ANGEL: Choose the way of Alice.

 FEELING THE PRESSURE: Solve all valve panel puzzles.

 **ULTIMATE STOMACHACHE:** Hunt down all Swollen Searchers.

 SPARE PARTS: Find all of Alice Angel's gears.

SOME ADDITIONAL EASTER EGGS!

- Hackers looking to peer behind some of the walled-off areas of this and other chapters have been met with this terrifying Bendy.

- In the stairwell directly above the sunken room, you'll see a boarded-off area above the wall. Between the boards you can see what appears to be a second Ink Machine that looks different from the main story version.

But before you return to Alice to finish *Chapter 3: Rise and Fall*, be sure to check the following items off your to-do list:

KNICK-KNACK PADDYWHACK: Get the poor doggie a bone (see page 50).

BLAZING METAL: Unleash the Tommy gun (see page 70).

TURN IT UP: Turn on the radio in Chapter 3, which appears in the stairwell on Level 11, near all the musical instruments.

NORMAN'S FATE: Bring down the Projectionist (see page 76).

INNER CHILD: Play with twenty-five Bendy dolls. You need only interact with the dolls—they'll make a squeaking sound.

BRING HOME THE BACON: Collect all Bacon Soup in Chapter 3 (see page 75).

LONG FORGOTTEN SELF: Listen to Henry's audio log (see page 77).

HEARING VOICES: Listen to all the audio logs in Chapter 3 (see page 75).

TEA TIME: Kick back with theMeatly. Head to Level P. In the small workshop room, to the right of the final valve puzzle you solved is a "Sheep Songs" poster. Walk through the wall to find theMeatly.

STUDIO LAYOUT

LEVEL K

LEVEL 9

LEVEL P

LEVEL 11

STAIRWELLS

BRIAR LABEL BACON SOUP

BRING HOME THE BACON

There are forty-two cans of Bacon Soup scattered throughout the studio in Chapter 3. Be sure to get them all for the "Bring Home the Bacon" Achievement.

LEVEL K

- Three cans, when you made Boris his Bacon Soup in the safehouse.
- One can, after opening the door to the safehouse, do not leave. Head back to the bathroom, where a previously locked stall on the left is now open. A can will be in the toilet.
- Four cans, three in front of the tall "Tasty Eats" crates, one between the "Tasty Eats" containers, obscured by cobwebs.
- One can, in the bottom of a shelving unit on your left.
- Two cans, on the floor around the corner from the previous shelf.
- One can, on a shelf at eye level, on your left.
- Two cans, on a desk to your right.

LEVEL 9

- One can, on the floor near a crate.
- One can, on the floor beside a pile of crates, obscured by a cobweb.

LEVEL 11

- Two cans, one on the crate in front of the door, another on the table.

LEVEL P

- One can, on the shelf beside the elevator.
- Four cans, one on a desk to the left of the doorway as you walk in, two on the crate to the left of the final valve puzzle, one on the floor beside the crate.

STAIRWELLS

- Eleven cans, in the stairwell above Level P, seven on a shelf loaded with bowls, four on a table beside a Little Miracle Station.
- One can, stairwell above Level 11, the desk on your left.
- Six cans, two stairwells above Level 11, on the floor to the right of a toilet.
- One can, stairwell below Level K, on top of a dresser, beside the ink cans.

HEARING VOICES

You'll need to listen to all the audio logs in this chapter for the "Hearing Voices" achievement:

- Shawn Flynn, Level K, alcove in the Heavenly Toys workshop
- Joey Drew, Level K, take the path of the Demon
- Susie Campbell, Level K, take the path of the Angel
- Wally Franks and Thomas Connor, Level K, before you hit the Butcher Gang poster, turn right into a new corridor
- Thomas Connor, Level 9, get off the elevator and go straight, descending the stairs toward Alice's domain
- Susie Campbell, Level 9, as you walk across the boards of the ink-flooded room, an audio log appears in the back right corner of the room
- Wally Franks, Level 11, just outside the room with the window
- Grant Cohen, Level 9, inside the boarded-up office
- Norman Polk, Level 14, on a crate just outside the Projectionist's domain
- Henry Stein, Level P, sunken room (see page 77)

New Objective:
COLLECT FIVE INK HEARTS

Take the elevator down to Level 14, where you'll encounter the Projectionist. You can avoid the Projectionist by staying out of his light while you gather the Ink Hearts. You can also choose to fight him, a difficult task, but one that will make gathering the hearts faster.

WEAPON	NUMBER OF HITS TO DEFEAT
GENT PIPE	72
TOMMY GUN	16
AXE	8

You can find the Ink Hearts in the following locations:

- The first Ink Heart appears in the hands of a dead Striker as you head out of the elevator.

- Take a left as you enter the Projectionist's domain. A second Ink Heart can be found in the hands of a dead Piper, across from a Little Miracle Station.

- Follow the path and continue straight to find a third Ink Heart near a dead Fisher.

- Continue on the path to find another Ink Heart on your right, near another dead Striker.

- Take a right at the forking path and continue straight until you hit a wall, and another dead Fisher, with the final Ink Heart.

Voice of
NORMAN POLK

Now I'm not lookin' for trouble. It's just the nature of us Projectionists to seek out the dark places.

You see, I've learned the ins and outs of this here studio. I know how to avoid being bothered by the likes of this . . . company.

That projectionist, they always say, creeping around, he's just lookin' for trouble. Well trouble or not, I see everything. They don't even know when I'm watchin'.

Even when I'm right behind 'em.

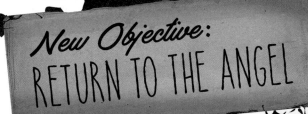

New Objective:
RETURN TO THE ANGEL

HENRY'S SECRET AUDIO LOG

After collecting all the Ink Hearts, exit the Projectionist's domain and head to the left of the stairs. You'll see an area that's been boarded off. Break through two sets of doors with the axe or Gent pipe to access a secret valve. Turn the valve to drain a secret corridor within the stairwell on Level P. Enter the Level P stairwell corridor (descending a flight of stairs) to hear a secret audio log from Henry.

Voice of HENRY

Only two weeks into this company and already it's gotten interesting. Joey is a man of ideas . . . And only ideas.

When I agreed to start this whole thing with him, I thought there would be a little more give and take. Instead I give, and he takes. I haven't seen Linda for days now.

Still, someone has to make this happen. When in doubt, just keep drawing, Henry.

On the plus side, I've got a new character I think people are going to love.

New Objective:
RETURN TO THE SURFACE

Once you're finished with everything you wanted to do, return to Alice on Level 9, placing the Ink Hearts in the drop box. Alice will instruct you to return to the lift for your reward.

Upon entering the lift, Alice will accuse you of stealing from her—revealing that she wants to sacrifice Boris to help make her beautiful again. Alice will quickly take the reins back on the elevator, plunging both you and Boris down below, where you will crash.

After coming to, you'll see Boris panicking, and Alice Angel walking behind him, before he is dragged away from you.

CHAPTER FOUR
"COLOSSAL WONDERS"

New Objective:
RESCUE BORIS

Studio Layout

Joey Drew Studios has a sprawling campus, and it's growing bigger by the day! You can use this helpful map to navigate.

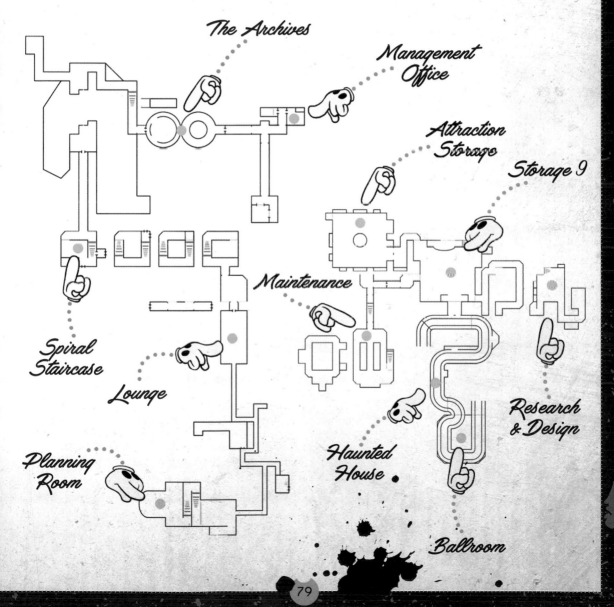

The Archives

Management Office

Attraction Storage

Storage 9

Spiral Staircase

Maintenance

Lounge

Research & Design

Planning Room

Haunted House

Ballroom

Accounting & Finance

As our Accounting & Finance Department is always reminding us, "Time is money," so we'll make this brief! Accounting & Finance handles the flow of money within our company, from the largest investments to the revenue generated by a single theater ticket. Unfortunately, all the dreaming we do here at Joey Drew Studios comes at a cost. New projects like Bendyland or the launching of a new character require a sizeable initial investment, which our accounting office balances against potential returns on that investment. That's a fancy way of saying that we have to spend money to make money.

Aside from managing revenue and investments, Accounting & Finance also handles many matters that directly affect your day to day. With mediation from the Administration Department, Accounting has final approval over department budgets, salaries, new hires, etc. Should you encounter any issues with your paycheck, your claim will likely go through Accounting with the help of Administration.

Whatever your concerns may be, if it's a money matter, it's likely under the jurisdiction of the dedicated staff of Accounting & Finance!

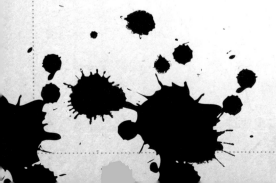

From: Grant Cohen, Accounting & Finance

RE: Employee Backpay

Valued Employee,

You are receiving this letter to notify you that you are owed BACKPAY IN THE AMOUNT OF $60.76. As our company awaits an influx of revenue from recent investments, we are unable to pay you. Rest assured that we are monitoring the situation closely and will offer you relief as soon as funds become available. We do not anticipate this period to last more than several weeks. Please feel free to visit Accounting & Finance on Level S with any further questions.

MacArthur Steel Co.
Quality Steel since 1874

23 Baker Street, Brooklyn, NY
Telephone 5-4855

Date June 23, 1944
Sold to Bertrum Piedmont, Joey Drew Studios

# Units	Item	Price	Amount
		Price	Amount
104	Industrial-Grade Steel	$47.39	$4,928.56
			$4,928.56
Total Debits			$0
Total Credits			$4,928.56
Net Sale			

Ticket No. 204-632

PAST DUE - 180 DAYS
PLEASE REMIT PAYMENT IMMEDIATELY

Receipts and Disbursements

July 1, 1944 to August 1, 1944

Receipts:

Investor Deposit, J. Dempsey	$24,800.00
Royalties, Heavenly Toys	$43,142.43
Box Office Sales	$56,879.18
Total Receipts	$124,821.61

Disbursements:

Employee Salaries	$56,659.74
Restocking Supplies	$18,982.50
Distribution Fees	$9,842.31
Marketing/Publicity	$10,372.12
Special Projects	$64,921.98
Taxes & Fees	$24,964.32
Total Disbursements	$185,742.97
Cash in Bank	$61,738.65
Balance as of August 2, 1944	$817.29

Mister Drew, we can't afford these high figures on special projects any longer. Please limit your spending or find additional investors — we're on the verge of being in the red again this year.

New Objective:
ENTER THE ARCHIVES

LEVEL **S**

ACCOUNTING & FINANCE

MANAGEMENT OFFICE

GRANT COHEN ▶

◀ ARCHIVES J-L

◀ R&D ACCESS

After waking up from the elevator crash, walk straight down the corridor until you reach the directory. The Archives are accessible via a door to the left, but the door is missing its valve. You'll need to find it.

Turn around and continue down the corridor toward the Accounting & Finance Management Office. The door on your left will be locked, but Grant Cohen's office, on the right, is open. Inside you'll find the door valve on the ground near a pipe on the far left wall. You may listen to the audio log here, but it'll be indiscernible. Return the valve to the door and enter the Archives.

BEFORE YOU GO...
After opening the door to the Archives, the door across from the Management Office will be unlocked. This room contains both a can of Bacon Soup and theMeatly!

Voice of
UNKNOWN

(Indiscernible)

From: Grant Cohen

To: Joey Drew

Mister Drew, I really do need to speak with you as soon as possible. Like I said in my last note, we're running $48,128 short this quarter. We won't be able to cover our taxes; I'm fielding daily calls from the IRS looking for our payments. There's not enough in the accounts right now to cover everything, even if I move some funds around and fudge the numbers. I've also received several sizeable bills from Gent, which I'll need to account for, besides the Bendyland payments, which we won't be able to make again this month. Can you please have your girl call down to me when you're next available?

The Archives

Established in 1929, Joey Drew Studios has been at the forefront of animation for more than a decade. Since the early talkies, our studio has been fueling the laughter and imagination of generations of children around the country. Never forget that you are a part of that legacy.

To that end, take some time before or after your shift to visit the Archives!

JOEY DREW STUDIOS TIMELINE

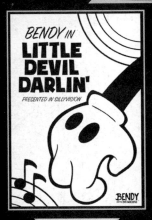

1929

Joey Drew Studios established by Joey Drew! Bendy premiered in his first cartoon, "Little Devil Darlin'," to the delight of children, many of whom had never seen a cartoon with sound before!

1929

Boris the Wolf premieres in "Sheep Songs!" The musical cartoon is an instant hit with fans, securing Boris a permanent spot in the Joey Drew family.

1933

Little girls around the country gain their own heroine when Alice Angel premieres in "Sent from Above"!

The Archives are your key to our company's history. Find out where we as a company came from, share your own story with the archivists, or peruse the thousands of rare company documents on display, including autographs from some of Hollywood's brightest stars! Our most valuable possessions are locked up tight in the finest safes from the Gent Corporation, so be sure to ask the archivists for assistance.

But beyond satisfying your curiosity about the studio, the Archives offer you an inexhaustible resource for knowledge about our cartoons. Here you'll find scripts from every cartoon ever created, reference for characters, even registries of ideas from meetings going back twelve years! Whether you're looking to explore a new angle for an upcoming short or searching for a "dancing chairs" visual reference, the Archives can help you with all your creative needs.*

*If you need to access the cartoons themselves, please visit the Film Vault to set up an appointment for viewing.

1934

Bendy is a household name! He and Boris get their own plush toys just in time for the holidays. Lines to buy these "Heavenly Toys" stretch outside the stores on Thirty-Fourth Street in New York City.

1935

Bendy finds himself in a bit of trouble when "The Butcher Gang" lands in theaters! These dastardly villains are always causing trouble for the little devil, but he finds a way to get back at them in the end.

1940

Joey Drew begins discussions with famed amusement-park designer Bertrum Piedmont on Bendyland, a state-of-the-art cartoon experience for families.

Voice of
SUSIE CAMPBELL

They told me I was perfect for the role. Absolutely perfect.

Now Joey's going around saying things behind closed doors.

I can always tell.

Now he wants to meet again tomorrow, says he has an "opportunity" for me.

I'll hear him out. But if that smooth talker thinks he can double-cross an angel and get away with it, well, oh he's got another thing coming.

Alice, ooh, she doesn't like liars.

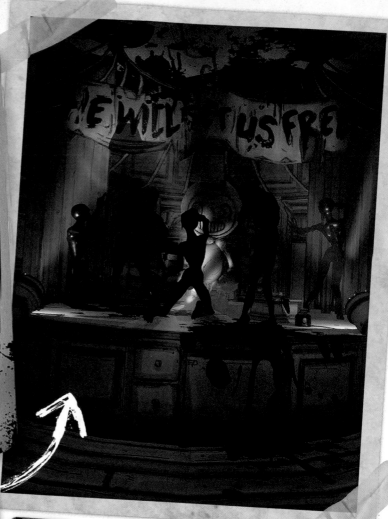

Directions:

Entering into the Archives, you'll see several inky figures clustered around a Bendy statue. These inky figures are called the Lost Ones. Once the music finishes playing, you'll get a new objective.

New Objective:
LOCATE THE SECRET PASSAGE

To locate the Secret Passage, head to the back of the next circular room. Push in the glowing book beside the door labeled "Private," and one of the lights above the door will turn on. You can keep track of how many books you've found by looking at the lightbulbs. When all the lightbulbs are on, you will be able to enter the Secret Passage. Push in four more books that are sticking out on the shelves: Two of them are located on the outer wall of the library room, and two are located on the inner wall. After pushing in the first three books, the screen will glitch for a moment, and the Lost Ones in the previous room will disappear.

New Objective:
ENTER THE DARKNESS

Through the Secret Passage you'll enter a dark cavern with a bridge. Interact with the lever to find that the bridge is missing a gear; you'll need to make a new gear to fix it.

New Objective:
REPAIR THE BRIDGE

Continue inside, to the safe-lined corridor. In the room at the end of the hall, pull the switch on your left to expose a well of ink. Turn the valve to summon a Swollen Searcher. Once the Searcher appears in the well, you'll be able to grab some of its thick ink and take it to the Ink Maker machine in the next room. Make sure the Ink Maker's dial on the right side of the machine is pointed to the gear that you want, then activate it and take the gear you've created to the bridge. This will grant you access to a bridge cart that will take you to the other side.

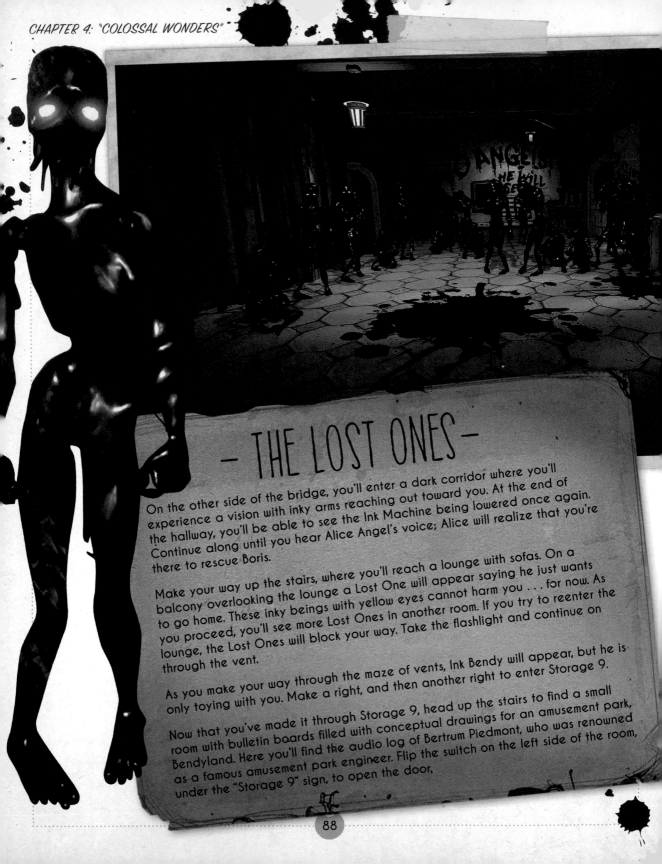

— THE LOST ONES —

On the other side of the bridge, you'll enter a dark corridor where you'll experience a vision with inky arms reaching out toward you. At the end of the hallway, you'll be able to see the Ink Machine being lowered once again. Continue along until you hear Alice Angel's voice; Alice will realize that you're there to rescue Boris.

Make your way up the stairs, where you'll reach a lounge with sofas. On a balcony overlooking the lounge a Lost One will appear saying he just wants to go home. These inky beings with yellow eyes cannot harm you . . . for now. As you proceed, you'll see more Lost Ones in another room. If you try to reenter the lounge, the Lost Ones will block your way. Take the flashlight and continue on through the vent.

As you make your way through the maze of vents, Ink Bendy will appear, but he is only toying with you. Make a right, and then another right to enter Storage 9.

Now that you've made it through Storage 9, head up the stairs to find a small room with bulletin boards filled with conceptual drawings for an amusement park, Bendyland. Here you'll find the audio log of Bertrum Piedmont, who was renowned as a famous amusement park engineer. Flip the switch on the left side of the room, under the "Storage 9" sign, to open the door,

NO ANGELS! HE WILL SET US FREE!

Voice of
BERTRUM PIEDMONT

For forty years, I've built attractions that stagger the imagination! Colossal wonders such as the world has never seen! I have earned my legacy with sweat.

But right in front of everyone... high level investors, Wall Street tycoons, the ever-tactless Joey Drew introduces me, the great Bertrum Piedmont, as Bertie! Like I was his child.

You may be paying me, Mister Drew! But you don't own me! I'll build you a park bigger than anything YOU could ever possibly conceive! But before you go taking any bows, Mister Drew, know that this grand achievement will belong to me... and to me alone.

JOEY DREW STUDIOS ANNOUNCES BENDYLAND

New York, NY—The world-renowned animators at Joey Drew Studios have been dreaming of their own amusement park for more than a decade now, and it seems those dreams are about to come true. Joey Drew Studios has just announced its newest endeavor: Bendyland. The massive amusement park, centered around the iconic Bendy and the studio's other animated creations, is slated to open sometime next year.

"Our mission is to bring dreams to everyday life," said Joey Drew, founder and president of the company. "We can think of no more perfect way to do that than to build an amusement park

designed for people of all ages. At Bendyland, imagination comes to life—literally."

Mister Drew wouldn't tell us more about when the groundbreaking will begin or where the amusement park will be

located, but public records have indicated several large tracts of the Meadowlands in southern New Jersey have been bought up by Drew's company.

Mister Drew was, however, quite forthcoming about the many attractions his park will feature. Bendyland will include motion rides, themed food and drink, and costumed characters. But aside from the basic midway fare, Drew insists there will be some major innovative surprises for fans of his films.

"For us, making Bendy real is important. The most important," continued Drew. "I was thrilled to hire Bertrum Piedmont for this task, or Bertie, as I like to call him. The amusement park is going swimmingly and I can't wait to unveil some of the colossal wonders we have in store for our fans."

Stay tuned for further updates on this exciting development.

Level S, Storage 9

If you have managed to gain employment at our studio, you likely already know about our exciting new endeavor: Bendyland! This amusement park for fans of all ages is sure to bring droves of families to our incredible cartoons, but right now, it's still in its early development.

To that end, Storage 9 and its adjacent Research & Design area on Level S are off-limits to all employees who are not stationed there for their daily work. This site contains active construction on several attractions, as well as cutting-edge technology that is considered unsafe for untrained hands. Please be sure to stay out of this area to avoid getting hurt.

Employees working in the warehouse are encouraged to wear the protective gear provided for them. Conditions in Storage 9 will likely change day to day as construction on Bendyland ramps up, so please remain alert and prepared to take on the tasks given to you. While it may be tempting, we ask our warehouse employees to refrain from playing games or interacting with unfinished rides due to safety concerns.

Regardless of your role in our company, we are excited to share more information about Bendyland as it develops. We may even have you, our valued employees, test out some of the attractions and games once they're ready for human contact! Until then, please stay safe.

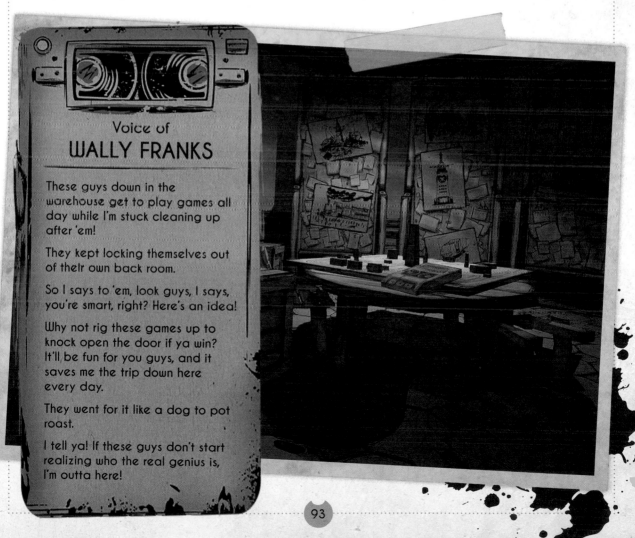

Voice of
WALLY FRANKS

These guys down in the warehouse get to play games all day while I'm stuck cleaning up after 'em!

They kept locking themselves out of their own back room.

So I says to 'em, look guys, I says, you're smart, right? Here's an idea!

Why not rig these games up to knock open the door if ya win? It'll be fun for you guys, and it saves me the trip down here every day.

They went for it like a dog to pot roast.

I tell ya! If these guys don't start realizing who the real genius is, I'm outta here!

New Objective:
POWER THE HAUNTED HOUSE

You'll enter a new room, a giant warehouse where all the Bendyland games, attractions, rides, etc., are stored. Head to the power station at the front of the room to get your new objective: Find four switches that power the Haunted House. You can follow the cords at the power station to find each switch.

To access the switches, you'll need to enter additional rooms, but the rooms are locked. You can access the first switch by winning the Bendyland mini-games. Once you win each mini-game, a sound cue will play (you don't need a perfect score), and a door will open at the foot of the stairs where you entered the warehouse.

Inside are three creepy Bendy mascot costumes, and the first switch.

Bendyland Mini-Games

Mister Drew, here are the game concepts for the midway, as requested. These will bring in quite a nice amount of revenue for the park.

STRENGTH TESTER

Classic strongman game. Pick up the mallet and hit the target to try to ring the bell. Your hit will be scored: "Weak!," "Man Baby!," "Brute!," and "Super!" This game has nothing to do with strength. It's all about timing.

BOTTLE WALLOP

Classic knock 'em down game. Take the three balls on the counter and toss them at three stacks of three bottles. Knock over all nine of the bottles in order to win the game. We'll make a killing here—players don't know that the bottles are specially weighted. They're best off aiming at the lower necks of the two bottom bottles.

BULL'S-EYE BONANZA

Use the toy gun to hit different targets as they appear; do not hit the targets with an "X" through them. Destroy all good targets in order to win. The speed of this will make it particularly difficult, plus the gun will only be loaded with enough bullets for the correct number of targets. Miss a shot, and you've already lost.

—RESEARCH & DESIGN—

Head back to the power station and flip the first switch. It will open the door to your left, to Research & Design. Here you'll find the Butcher Gang, standing around a burning barrel below. You must throw the empty Bacon Soup cans to lure them away to another part of the room while you slip by. Note that these enemies cannot be defeated with the empty cans until after you throw the second switch and open the door to leave the area.

You'll find the second power switch by taking a left at the burning barrel. Back here you'll find another Lost One in a caged-off room. Continue back into the workshop, where there is a half-finished, animatronic Bendy, and an audio log from Lacie Benton.

Voice of
LACIE BENTON

The only thing that works around here is my ulcer. Half these people don't know a wrench from a dang steamroller. Buncha morons is what they are. Spend their day in the warehouse arguin' over who's supposed to be doin' what or playing them silly games. Still, I'm not complainin'. I get most of my time to myself. Suits me just fine. Only thing that bothers me is that mechanical demon in the corner. Bertrum's been working on it for a month now. Says it will walk someday and maybe dance. All it does now is give me the creeps. I swear, when my back's turned . . . that thing's movin'.

THE CREATOR LIED TO US.

Directions:

Before returning upstairs, you'll need to throw a switch to open the door again. This time, hang a right at the burning barrel to locate the switch, then return to the warehouse.

NO. dream bigger.

But can
we make it even
more lifelike?

Directions:

Throw the second switch at the power station to open the door to "Attraction Storage."

After winding your way along the corridor, you'll come to a big open room with a ride in the center. Play the audio log on the table and get ready for a fight.

THE BIGGEST PARK EVER BUILT, A CENTERFOLD OF ATTRACTIONS. EACH ONE MORE GRAND THAN THE ONE BEFORE IT. IT MAKES MY EYES COME TO TEARS AT THE THOUGHT. BUT THEN... OH, MISTER DREW. FOR ALL YOUR TALK OF DREAMS, YOU ARE THE TRUE ARCHITECT BEHIND SO MANY NIGHTMARES. I BUILT THIS PARK. IT WAS TO BE A MASTERPIECE! MY MASTERPIECE! AND NOW YOU THINK YOU CAN JUST THROW ME OUT? TRAMPLE ME TO THE DUST AND FORGET ME? NO! THIS IS MY PARK! MY GLORY! YOU MAY THINK I'VE GONE... BUT I'M STILL HERE!

Directions:

Once the audio log is over, Bertrum will smash the desk in front of you. In the shards of the desk you'll find an axe. Wield the axe against the glowing joints on the arms of the ride. Bertrum will throw his arms around, smashing one against the ground until it goes limp. That is your chance to move in and hack off the joint screws (four per arm). Once all four joint screws are off, the arm will break. Hack off the four joint screws on all four limbs to defeat Bertrum. Once he's defeated you will lose your axe, but you will be able to unlock the third power switch.

THE MAD HOUSE

DARL'N DUCK BOATS

5
BENDYLAND RA

FUN

OFFICES

LIGHT LAND

BIG LAND

DARK LAND

TINY LAND

WEST ENTRANCE

EAST ENTRANCE

MAIN ENTRANCE

BENDYLAND
RIDE TICKET
ADMISSION TO ONE RIDE
1961

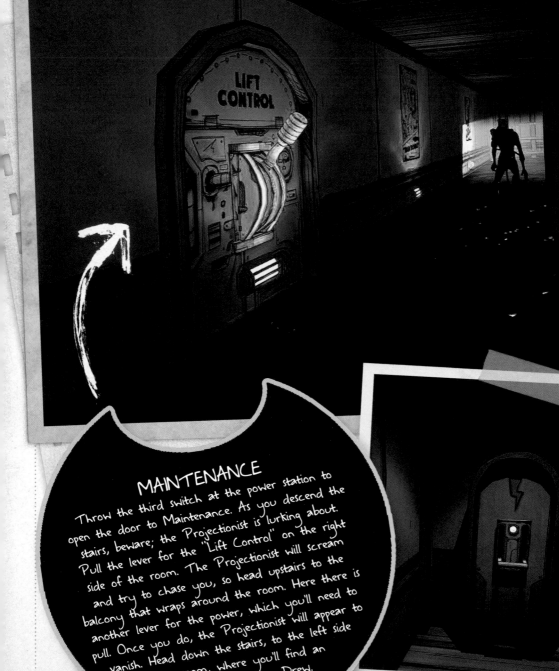

MAINTENANCE

Throw the third switch at the power station to open the door to Maintenance. As you descend the stairs, beware; the Projectionist is lurking about. Pull the lever for the "Lift Control" on the right side of the room. The Projectionist will scream and try to chase you, so head upstairs to the balcony that wraps around the room. Here there is another lever for the power, which you'll need to pull. Once you do, the Projectionist will appear to vanish. Head down the stairs, to the left side of the room, where you'll find an audio log from Joey Drew.

Directions:

Continue back up the steps toward the exit, but the exit is locked. The Projectionist will pursue you, so hide in the Little Miracle Station, where you will watch Bendy destroy the Projectionist right in front of you. When the scene is over, you'll be able to exit and activate the final switch at the power station in the warehouse.

Voice of
JOEY DREW

I believe there's something special in all of us. With true inner strength, you can conquer even your biggest challenges. You just have to believe in yourself and remain honest, motivated, and above all, who you really are.

Okay, let's stop it right there. I can only do so many takes of this trash a day. And tell the guys in writing I want more use of the word *dreaming* in every message. Keep railing on that, get it? Dreaming! Dreaming! Dreaming! People just eat up that kind of slop. Hmm. What? It's still on? Well, turn it off, damn it!

OVERACHIEVER!

A few achievements will be given to you through the natural course of the story:

 AROUND AND AROUND: Defeat Bertrum Piedmont.

 HAUNTING WE WILL GO: Restore power to the Haunted House.

 REUNITED: Find Boris.

But before you head inside the Haunted House to finish *Chapter 4: "Colossal Wonders,"* be sure to check the following items off your to-do list:

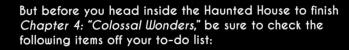 BARBECUED: Visit theMeatly. (You can find him in the room opposite Grant Cohen's office. Walk through the "Sheep Songs" poster on the wall. Unlike other chapters, where you cannot access him until near the end of the chapter, you can visit theMeatly as soon as you unlock the Archives door.)

FINGER WAGGIN': Turn on the radio in Chapter 4. (In the caverns outside the Archives, use the Ink Maker machine to create a radio. Turn it on to gain this achievement.)

WASTING TIME: Ring the bell. (Get a "Super!" on the Strength Tester mini-game.)

BULL'S-EYE: Get a perfect score on the Bull's-Eye Bonanza mini-game.

CALL THE MILK MAN: Get a perfect score on the Bottle Wallop mini-game.

GOING TO BE SICK: Go for a wild ride. (While fighting Bertrum, wait until he lays his arm down, then try to interact with the cart. Doing so will allow you to ride without dying. Don't get sick!)

A LITTLE SOUVENIR: Take a photo at the photo cutout. (In the Maintenance room, climb the stairs to the walkway above the inky floor. There you'll find a cardboard cutout of a figure with a trident. Walk behind it and look through the hole at the camera, which will snap a photo.)

STILL LISTENING: Listen to all the audio logs in Chapter 4 (see page 108).

JUST LIKE MOM USED TO MAKE: Collect all the Bacon Soup in Chapter 4 (see page 107).

UNLIKELY VICTORY: Complete Chapter 4 with the plunger (see page 109).

STUDIO LAYOUT

BRIAR LABEL
BACON
SOUP

JUST LIKE MOM USED TO MAKE

There are nineteen cans of Bacon Soup scattered throughout the studio in Chapter 4. Be sure to get them all for the "Just Like Mom Used to Make" achievement.

- One can, on the floor to your right outside the elevator.
- One can, in the trash bin. (This door will unlock after you open the Archives door.)
- One can, on the floor behind a TV, beside a desk.
- One can, to the left of the inky well where the Swollen Searcher appears.
- One can, at eye level on a shelf to your right as you ascend the stairs.
- One can, inside the trunk to the left of the doorway.
- One can, on the floor between a crate and a bulletin board.
- One can, on the ledge of an empty games booth, to the right of the Bottle Wallop.
- Two cans, one on the railing to the right of the door as you enter, another on the barrel near the first can, surrounded by empty cans.

- One can, lying on its side on top of the first shelving unit as you enter the animatronic workshop.
- Two cans, one to the right of a dead Striker, another opposite the Striker, on top of a crate.
- Two cans, one to the left as you walk in, hidden behind a barrel, another to the left of the giant mouth, on a crate.
- One can, under the "Buddy Boris Railway" poster, under one of the pistons.
- One can, on top of a barrel in the corner, on the balcony.
- One can, as you enter the Haunted House, search under the seat of one of the empty carts to your right.
- One can, on the table, to the left of the pipe organ.

—STILL LISTENING—

You'll need to listen to all the audio logs in this chapter for the "Still Listening" achievement:

- Unknown, Grant Cohen's office
- Susie Campbell, second Archives room
- Bertrum Piedmont, Bendyland concept room, before Bendyland warehouse
- Wally Franks, Bendyland warehouse, between Bottle Wallop and Bull's-Eye Bonanza
- Lacie Benton, Research & Design, animatronic room
- Bertrum Piedmont, Attractions, Bertrum's room
- Joey Drew, Maintenance, Projectionist's lair

—ARM YOURSELF!—

- GENT PIPE: If you don't take any of the below steps, you will face the final boss with the Gent pipe.

- PLUNGER: After you pull the fourth lever to access the Haunted House, return to Maintenance. Descend the stairs to the inky abyss, then head upstairs to the balcony area. To the left of the power lever is a chest; open it and retrieve the dial inside. During the final battle of Chapter 4, interact with the Ink Maker, which will have a new setting to make the plunger.

- EMPTY BACON SOUP CANS: After you pull the second lever for the Haunted House, return to the Research & Design animatronic room, where you can stock up on as many as thirty one empty Bacon Soup cans in the shelves across from the Bendy animatronic. You can take these out of the room and use them to defeat the final boss (or any other enemy in Chapter 4) without the hassle of the Ink Maker. Defeating the final boss in this way will trigger a flashing hallucination.

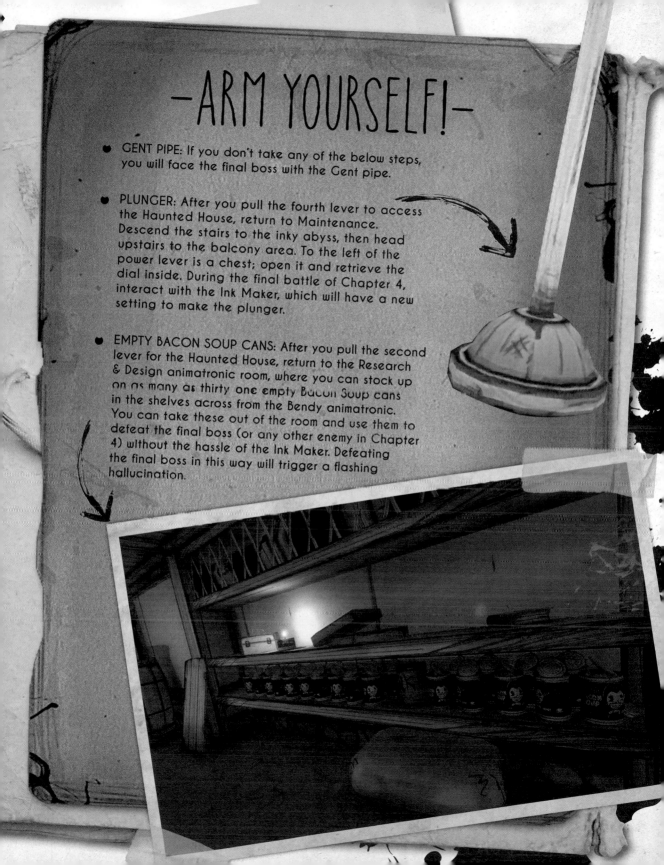

New Objective: DEFEAT BORIS

—INSIDE THE HAUNTED HOUSE—

With all switches activated, the Haunted House opens! You will need to get into a roller-coaster cart in order to proceed, despite passing a "Turn Back" sign.

After boarding, you'll hear Alice Angel's voice, taunting you for wanting to rescue Boris. When she's done speaking, you'll enter a massive, dimly lit room with sofas, barrels, and a warmly lit chandelier. Here you'll be reunited with Boris, but Alice has modified him a bit. It is now your task to defeat this "new and improved" Brute Boris.

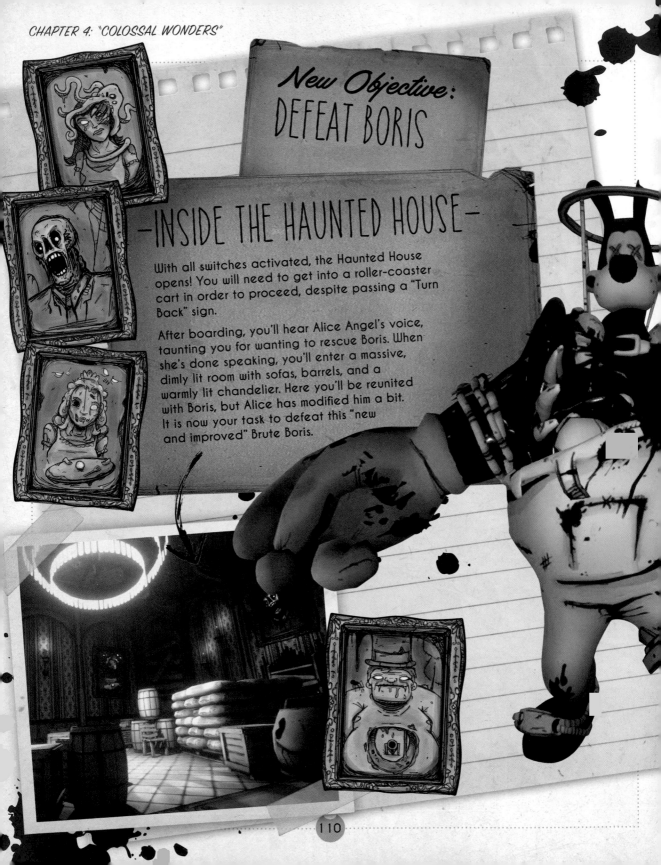

—BRINGING DOWN BRUTE BORIS—

1. Dodge Brute Boris's attacks as he runs into the walls, trying to attack you. Beware: Two hits from him will land you at the respawn point.

2. He'll start bleeding ink for a few seconds. Stop and collect the thick ink that Brute Boris leaves behind.

3. Use the Ink Maker and the thick ink to create the Gent pipe or plunger if you retrieved the special gear.

4. When Brute Boris runs into another wall and bleeds again, hit him with your weapon. Any weapons made with the Ink Maker are good for one use only, so your weapon will break after a strike.

5. Brute Boris will now start jumping about the room, trying to smash you. Again, two hits will bring you down.

6. Wait until Brute Boris starts bleeding ink again, collect it, and put it into the Ink Maker to create a new weapon. Hit him while he is bleeding. Your weapon will disappear again.

7. Brute Boris will now pick up roller-coaster carts as they enter the room and try to throw them at you. If one cart hits you, you will die.

8. Dodge the carts, wait until he starts bleeding, and collect his ink. Put it into the Ink Maker to make your final weapon. One more hit will bring Brute Boris down for good.

Once the battle is over, you will encounter two new figures—a blade-wielding angel and someone who looks very much like Boris used to.

If you gave Boris a bone in Chapter 3, and played straight through to Chapter 4, Brute Boris will still have the bone in his mouth.

CHAPTER FIVE
"THE LAST REEL"

HOPE

Studio Layout

Joey Drew Studios has a sprawling campus, and it's growing bigger by the day! You can use this helpful map to navigate.

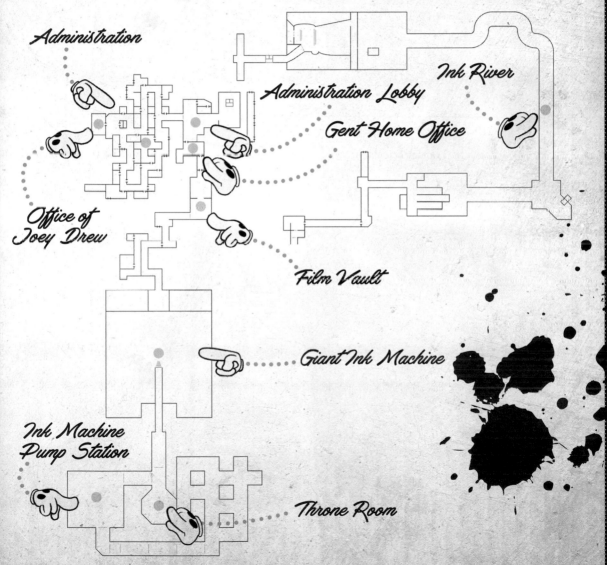

Administration

Administration Lobby

Ink River

Gent Home Office

Office of Joey Drew

Film Vault

Giant Ink Machine

Ink Machine Pump Station

Throne Room

Mr. & Mrs. Frederick Pendle request
the honor of your presence at the marriage
of their daughter,

Allison

to

Mr. Thomas J. Connor

on Saturday, the twenty-third day of February
nineteen hundred and fifty-two
at two-thirty in the afternoon
at First Light Presbyterian Church

Reception to follow

Joey,
You and your studio brought us together. You should
be with us on our wedding day. Hope you'll join us.
—Allison

Mister Joey Drew

X Regretfully declines
____ Will attend

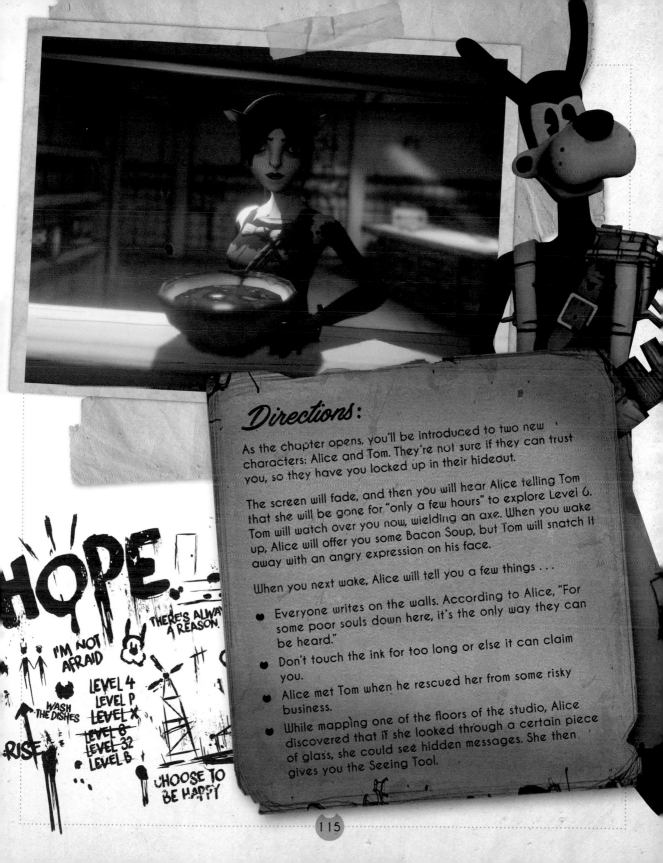

Directions:

As the chapter opens, you'll be introduced to two new characters: Alice and Tom. They're not sure if they can trust you, so they have you locked up in their hideout.

The screen will fade, and then you will hear Alice telling Tom that she will be gone for "only a few hours" to explore Level 6. Tom will watch over you now, wielding an axe. When you wake up, Alice will offer you some Bacon Soup, but Tom will snatch it away with an angry expression on his face.

When you next wake, Alice will tell you a few things . . .

- Everyone writes on the walls. According to Alice, "For some poor souls down here, it's the only way they can be heard."
- Don't touch the ink for too long or else it can claim you.
- Alice met Tom when he rescued her from some risky business.
- While mapping one of the floors of the studio, Alice discovered that if she looked through a certain piece of glass, she could see hidden messages. She then gives you the Seeing Tool.

HOPE

THERE'S ALWAYS A REASON.

I'M NOT AFRAID

WASH THE DISHES

LEVEL 4
LEVEL P
LEVEL X
LEVEL 8
LEVEL 32
LEVEL B

RISE

CHOOSE TO BE HAPPY

— WIELDING THE SEEING TOOL —

Alice will hand you the Seeing Tool, which you can use to discover hidden messages. Move around to reveal secrets in this scene.

- "She will leave you for dead" is written on the wall behind Alice.

- A halo around Alice's head

After using the Seeing Tool, Alice will admit that she thinks she isn't meant to leave the studio, but perhaps you are— she thinks you might be "the hope I've been waiting for."

Alice will tell you to sleep and wake up tomorrow. The screen will fade, and later you'll hear Alice arguing with Tom. Tom did something rash to alert Ink Bendy of their location. A little while later, Ink Bendy has found the hideout. Although Alice will try to free you from the barricade, she won't be able to, and Alice and Tom will leave.

SHE
WILL
LEAVE
YOU
FOR
DEAD

YOU DRAW
BEAUTIFULLY

New Objective:
ESCAPE YOUR PRISON

Use your Seeing Tool to reveal more secrets in the room. Bring it to the right and you will spot messages reading:

- "It's inside the vault!"
- "Let me out of here!"
- "So many questions."
- "Trust her."
- "Spoon"
- "Don't go through the door."
- "What door?"

You will also see various drawings, including a coffin on your cot.

Move your Seeing Tool over more of the wall and you'll notice directions to take a spoon that is hanging on the wall. When you do, a secret passageway to a bathroom will be revealed. Use your Seeing Tool to discover a prompt to look inside the toilet tank. Lift the lid off the tank and take the Gent pipe that has been hidden inside.

Use the Gent pipe to break away the boards in the doorway. You can use the Seeing Tool to discover more hidden messages in this room.

Leave the hideout, walking along the plank bridge, defeating Searchers as you encounter them.

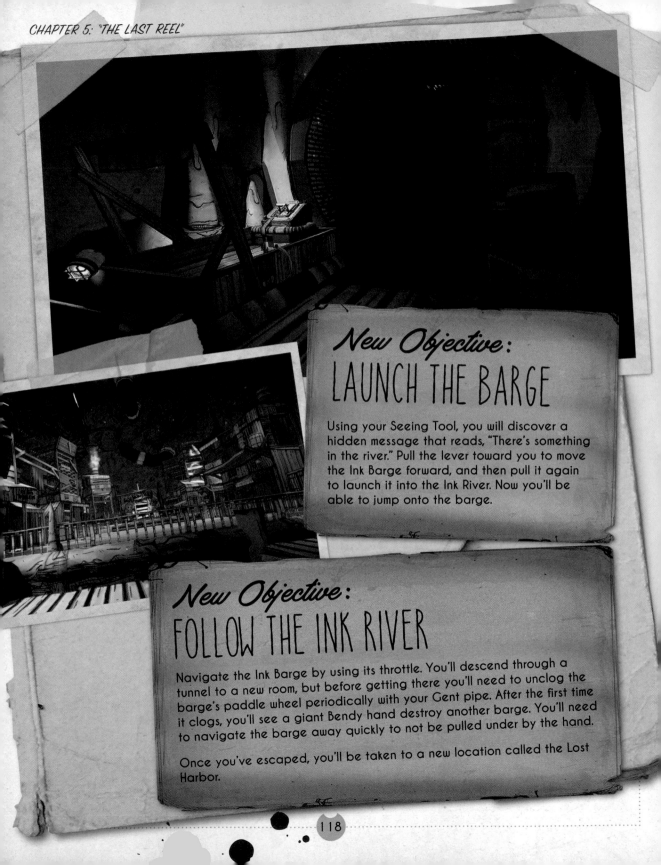

New Objective:
LAUNCH THE BARGE

Using your Seeing Tool, you will discover a hidden message that reads, "There's something in the river." Pull the lever toward you to move the Ink Barge forward, and then pull it again to launch it into the Ink River. Now you'll be able to jump onto the barge.

New Objective:
FOLLOW THE INK RIVER

Navigate the Ink Barge by using its throttle. You'll descend through a tunnel to a new room, but before getting there you'll need to unclog the barge's paddle wheel periodically with your Gent pipe. After the first time it clogs, you'll see a giant Bendy hand destroy another barge. You'll need to navigate the barge away quickly to not be pulled under by the hand.

Once you've escaped, you'll be taken to a new location called the Lost Harbor.

– THE LOST HARBOR –

Use your Seeing Tool to discover a hidden message that reads, "Once people, now fallen into despair." Another hidden message says, "You bring death."

By navigating closely to the barricaded door you'll trigger Sammy Lawrence, who breaks down the barriers and comes after you with an axe. You'll need to dodge his attacks and use the Gent pipe to knock his mask off his face. Approach him again and he will throw you to the ground, after which Alice and Tom will rescue you.

After Sammy Lawrence fades away, Tom will offer you an axe. Hordes of Searchers, Miner Searchers, and Lost Ones will spawn to attack you. (For the first time, these Lost Ones are enemies and can harm you.) Destroy them all with your axe; Alice and Tom will help you.

ENEMY	NUMBER OF HITS TO DEFEAT
SEARCHER	1
LOST ONE	2
MINER SEARCHER	4

This will be a lengthy battle, but when it's over, Alice will ask you to lead the way out.

To escape the Lost Harbor, use your axe to break down the barriers on the path to the left of where Sammy Lawrence emerged.

1946   **— WEEKLY**

JOEY DREW STUDIOS UNDER INVESTIGATION
FINANCIAL TROUBLE LOOMING FOR ANIMATION COMPANY

New York, NY—Joey Drew Studios is under investigation, with former employees citing hazardous work environments, harassment, and excessive backpay. The company is also in danger of going bankrupt, according to investors.

"These accusations are preposterous—they're ridiculous," said Joey Drew, founder and president of the company. "I vehemently deny them. These are sad lies no doubt made by disgruntled former employees or competing studios. Our facility is state-of-the-art. Joey Drew Studios is where dreams happen. And it's where dreams are going to happen. We have no financial troubles at all."

Anonymous workers at Joey Drew Studios have threatened to unionize over the poor conditions, which include unpermitted building, hazardous electrical wiring, and a plumbing system prone to bursting. Many employees also cite excessive work hours, most of which were unpaid. Several animators confided that they hadn't seen their families in weeks, after being threatened with disciplinary action and termination if they were unable to finish animations on exceedingly tight schedules.

Music director Sammy Lawrence seemed unfazed by the claims. "Joey runs a pretty tight ship. Some people can't take it, and that's fine. This industry is all about survival of the fittest. We don't need a bunch of useless sheep who can't finish their work on time."

Despite the mounting evidence against the company, Mister Drew remains adamant that the studio has done nothing wrong.

"I am so certain that there's nothing wrong with our studio, I not only welcome

WSPAPER

PRICE THREE CENTS

investigators—I invite them," said Drew. "Reports of barricaded offices, employees locked in work spaces, and malfunctioning machinery are just crazy. And about the money, why, we just installed new technology in partnership with the Gent Corporation! We certainly wouldn't have done that if we were going bankrupt! In fact, we're on the verge of taking our business to the next level. I can't wait to show everyone what we have in store with our new cartoons."

City officials have reported that they will be exploring these complaints against the company in the coming weeks, to determine if the claims have any merit. In the meantime, employees seem to be fleeing the studio in droves. Recent job listings have included a head of animation, several background and character artists, as well as inkers and storyboard artists. If his staffing issues are as bad as they seem, one must wonder if Mister Drew intends to draw future cartoons himself.

Voice of
JOEY DREW

A small memo to all administration offices!

Rumors have begun to fly that we simply can't tolerate any longer. The idea that the company is in some form of financial difficulty is untrue and a slanderous lie against us.

It's also been known to me that some backroom incompetents are not trusting in my leadership.

As a leader, I'm always steering the boat, guiding our destiny. Looking at the big picture. No need for you people to worry about such complicated things. Just do whatever it is you do and trust your leader . . . which is me.

▲ INK WELL

■ LITTLE MIRACLE STATION

✖ INK MAKER MACHINE

New Objective:
DRAIN THE PASSAGE

Next you'll be led into a new location with upbeat music playing, the Administration offices. You'll need to obtain missing pipes in order to drain the passage to the Film Vault.

To get these pipes, you'll need to:

1. Open the door to Administration. To do this, turn right at the Ink Maker machine in the corner of the lobby, then head through two doorways until you're behind the lobby desk. Pull the switch to open the door.

2. Collect thick ink, which you can find at the inky fountain outside the office of Joey Drew.

3. Return to the Ink Maker machine in the Administration lobby. Insert the thick ink into the Ink Maker.

4. Select the proper pipe icon on the Ink Maker's dial and turn the wheel. Tip: You will need a "T" pipe, a straight pipe, and a bent pipe, so make sure to turn the dial to the correct setting.

5. Head to the Film Vault entrance and insert the missing pipe into the piping system.

6. If you're pursued by the Butcher Gang, you can try to lose them in the maze of offices, head to a Little Miracle Station, or run into the pool of ink at the start of this area.

When all the pipes are restored, the Film Vault door will open.

Administration

Feeling a bit turned around? You must have wandered into the Administration offices! Like the oil in a finely tuned machine, Administration provides the grease that keeps our company running smoothly. Our talented administrative staff handle many vital functions to our company, such as:

- Keeping the company well stocked with supplies needed by various departments.

- Acting as mediator between Accounting and different departments to come to a healthy compromise on all budgetary concerns.

- Processing job postings, new hires, and keeping current employees happy and content in their role at our studio.

- Liaising with external companies such as Gent Corporation and Briar Label Co., and exploring new avenues for corporate partnership.

- Managing paperwork and developing new methods to make our staff even more productive.

If you should ever have a concern that falls under one of the above areas, feel free to swing by the Administrative offices. But be warned—it's a bit of a maze down here! You might want to call ahead and ask for directions.

TODAY'S APPOINTMENTS

PLEASE SIGN IN AT FRONT DESK ON ARRIVAL.
NO APPOINTMENT. NO ACCESS.

9:30	Dr. Hackenbush DVM
10:00	Bertrum Piedmont (rescheduled)
10:15	F. Fontaine
11:15	Health & Safety Board Agent
11:30	E. Misner – PP
11:45	Sammy Lawrence
12:00	Mr. Drew at lunch!
2:00	Thomas Connor – GENT
2:15	Charles and the Prodigies
2:45	M.M. meeting (out of office)
3:30	That Puppet Guy
5:30	Hayden – UAC
6:00	Susie Campbell

JOEY DREW STUDIOS

Voice of
WALLY FRANKS

So turns out it's my lucky day! I got to cleaning some of the offices around 2 a.m. last night. And what do you think I find on one of the chairs? A big freaking chocolate cake. Just sitting there! Practically yelling my name!

You know? I work hard! I earn my pay. Every darn dollar. But you know what this company's missing? Little, benefitting perks. And this here cake? It's a perk!

Hopefully no one finds out what I done. 'Cause if they did, I can tell what would happen. I'm outta here.

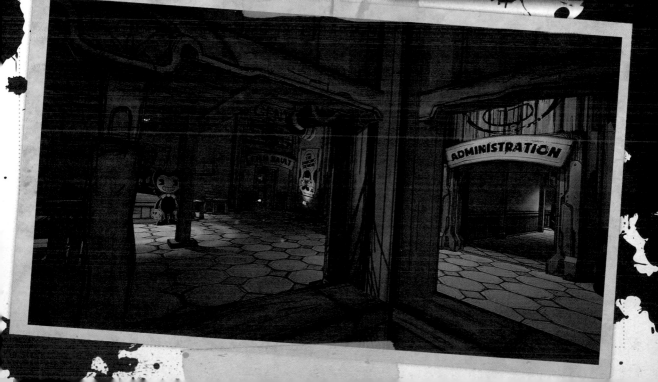

Our Friends at

Besides Briar Label Co., the company name you'll likely hear thrown around the studio most is Gent Corporation. After sponsoring the hit "Construction Corruption" Bendy and Boris cartoon, a truly magnificent partnership was born between Joey Drew Studios and the Gent Corporation. Our state-of-the-art studio is a testament to the innovative, can-do attitude of Gent and its employees. (And their low, low pricing helps too!)

From the elevators you likely ride each morning to the safes being locked up in the Archives each night; the valves and pipes that keep our plumbing flowing to the flashlights our handyman might use to find a blown fuse, Gent keeps this studio going day in and day out. In addition to everyday devices, Gent has also created several machines of the future, including the Ink Maker machines. With the crank of a handle this technology can spit out a functioning item made from high-quality, thick ink. Whether you need a pipe, a gear, a plunger, or a radio, the Ink Maker can build it for you at little to no cost to our company!

Best of all, Gent staff are always on call to help whenever a pipe bursts or the lights go out or you have a new machine in mind that can help increase your department's productivity!

Voice of
THOMAS CONNOR

Progress Report to the Gent Home Office.

Client: Joey Drew Studios.

Although we're making progress, the client's expectations keep changing. What started as a machine to simply mold life-size figures now seems to be teetering on the edge of magic more than engineering.

Although Mister Drew remains convinced they are the same thing.

The process of running the cartoon film through the machine for the figures to imprint upon themselves is going well. We've had several near successes.

One weird note, the first figure ever created was a foiled attempt in the likeness of the character called Bendy. Since that time, no other attempts of this particular figure have emerged. And the one that did, I dunno, there's just something unworldly about him.

Voice of
JOEY DREW

Listen, Tommy, I know you boys over at Gent are doing your best, but I'm paying for living attractions, not weird abominations!

Whatever that grinning thing was I saw wandering around your office, you better keep it locked up tight!

I realize it was a first attempt but imagine if the press caught sight of it! Might scare off investors!

And in response to your previous memo: If you claim your failures are because these things are soulless, then, damn it, we'll get them a soul!

After all, I own thousands of 'em!

BENDY and BO

CONST

COR

Office of
Joey Drew

ince Bendy first sprang to life from Mister Joey Drew's pen in 1929, the founder and president of Joey Drew Studios has kept our business running full-steam to the forefront of animation. An accomplished animator, most of Mister Drew's time today is spent meeting with new investors and various department heads so he can best continue to steer the company on the right course.

Mister Drew keeps his office in Administration and makes it a priority

ATTENTION!

JOEY DREW STUDIOS IS NOT INTERESTED IN THE AQUIRING OF NEW PROPERTIES THAT ARE DERIVATIVES OF EXISTING CHARACTERS.

FOR BEST PITCH:

- BE EARLY FOR YOUR APPOINTMENT

- KEEP PITCH UNDER THREE MINUTES

- HAVE YOUR PITCH FEE CHECK READY

to remain accessible to his employees. If you'd like to make a one-on-one appointment, you can contact his secretary at any time. That said, you're more likely to run into Mister Drew around the studio, adjusting a storyboard in animation or attending a voice-over session in the recording booths. As the creator of Bendy, Boris the Wolf, and Alice Angel, Mister Drew views these characters and his employees as his family, and he always makes time for family. Mister Drew enjoys staying active and involved with the day-to-day happenings at his studio, so if you see him around, share something about your job that you're excited about. Better yet, share one of your dreams with him. It is Mister Drew's sincerely held belief that the lifeblood of innovation comes from the kind of crazy concepts that more pragmatic people might cast aside. Mister Drew loves to say that he got started with just "a pencil and a dream." The pencil was important, but the dream is what built this studio and continues to drive its success.

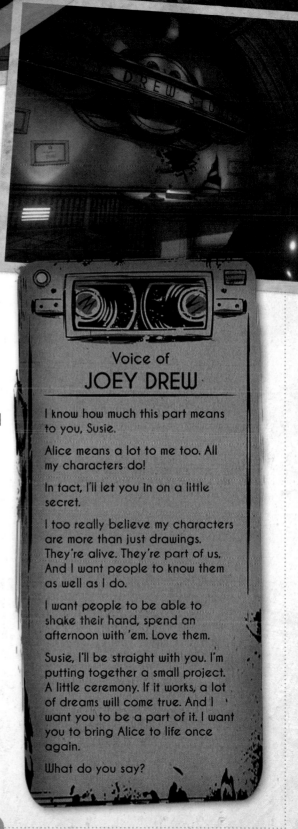

Voice of
JOEY DREW

I know how much this part means to you, Susie.

Alice means a lot to me too. All my characters do!

In fact, I'll let you in on a little secret.

I too really believe my characters are more than just drawings. They're alive. They're part of us. And I want people to know them as well as I do.

I want people to be able to shake their hand, spend an afternoon with 'em. Love them.

Susie, I'll be straight with you. I'm putting together a small project. A little ceremony. If it works, a lot of dreams will come true. And I want you to be a part of it. I want you to bring Alice to life once again.

What do you say?

Welcome to the
Film Vault!

If you're looking to watch one of the hundreds of Bendy, Boris the Wolf, or Alice Angel cartoons made right here in our studio, you've come to the right place! The Film Vault is your resource for the many hours of animated footage produced in Joey Drew Studios' fifteen-plus years of operation. Most of these films are no longer in theaters, and some have been out of circulation for years.

To schedule an appointment to review footage, simply call the office of our projectionist, Norman Polk. Mr. Polk would be pleased to assist you with reviewing whatever footage you require. You can peruse some of their fine selections on the next pages!

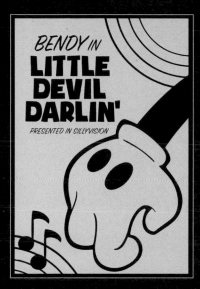

The first Bendy cartoon, "Little Devil Darlin'," helped to cement Bendy's place in the hearts of fans.

Another oldie "The Dancing Demon" was recently re-released (along with many other of our classics) in concert with the US government in an effort to raise sales on war bonds.

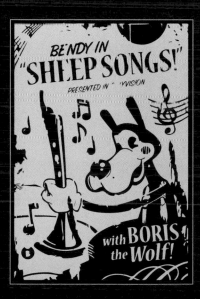

The first animated feature starring everyone's best buddy, Boris! Fans loved the interactions between Bendy and Boris so much that Boris became a regular cast member in Joey Drew Studios' cartoons.

This popular animated feature from the early days of the studio spawned its own line of popular toy trains from Heavenly Toys!

In 1933, the world was introduced to Alice Angel in "Sent from Above." Joey Drew Studios' own singing, dancing angel stole hearts around the country.

"Bendy and Boris Go to Hell in a Hand Basket" was our studio's first foray into longer-form animation. This cartoon featured an extended runtime as the iconic duo rides a mine cart through a dark and spooky underworld.

"Siren Serenade" was the first Alice Angel cartoon that did not feature any other Joey Drew cast members such as Bendy or Boris.

A dash of spice makes all the difference in this comedic Bendy feature from the early 1930s.

It was Bendy to the rescue in "Hellfire Fighter"!

Bendy met his first recurring villains in "The Butcher Gang"! Charley, Barley, and Edgar would never pass up an opportunity to pick on anyone—let alone a little devil like Bendy—but they get their comeuppance in the end!

Bendy was juggling more than just flaming batons in this 1937 cartoon feature.

Bendy was out for fame and glory in "Showbiz Bendy," a cartoon that saw him teaming up with Alice and Boris on a magic act on Broadway's biggest stage.

Avast ye scallywags! Bendy explored the ocean blue in "The Devil's Treasure," where he sought out a pirate's secret booty.

The Butcher Gang returned in "Demonic Tonic," in which the nefarious villains shrunk
Bendy, trapping him in a bottle for their own amusement.

Bendy was on nanny duty in "Rosemary's Baby-Sitter."

Just in time for the nation's Halloween festivities, "Tombstone Picnic" debuted to send a shiver down America's spine. Bendy even came face to face with

This wintertime mini-short became a holiday classic for families around the country. Poor Bendy tries to make the perfect snowman.

Following up on the earlier success of "Tombstone Picnic," "Haunted Hijinx" saw Bendy and Boris reunited for more frightening fare!

New Objective:
SEARCH THE VAULT

Once inside the vault, you'll be able to search around. Interact with the glowing box to reveal a set of tangled film reels inside. Then you'll be reunited with Alice and Tom, who used a rope to get down to the Film Vault.

Here, you reveal that Ink Bendy has something you need. You'll have to enter the Demon's lair to get it. While Alice lists off the things you'll need to find to break through the door to your right, Tom will punch the door open with brute force. You'll enter a new corridor that will seem familiar . . . You'll come upon a Bendy cutout, and nearby it is a solitary desk: yours.

Then you'll turn the corner (ignoring the painted ink that reads "Death" with an arrow pointing that way) and come upon the sprawling Ink Machine Room. Alice tells you that she and Tom can't wade their way through the ink river because they'll disappear . . . but you can.

OVERACHIEVER!

A few achievements will be given to you through the natural course of the story:

PIPES AND PROBLEMS: Create and place all the missing pipes to drain the passage to the Film Vault.

SHADOWS AND SUFFERING: Discover what's living below. (Finish fighting the Searchers and Lost Ones in the Lost Harbor.)

TO HELL AND BACK: Complete the main story.

But before you wade into the Ink Machine to finish *Chapter 5: "The Last Reel,"* be sure to check the following items off your to-do list:

GOLDBRICKING: Let others do the work. (When you're set upon by Searchers, don't help Alice and Tom kill them for a while.)

VALUED EMPLOYEE: Take a longer walk. (While collecting pipe segments in Administration, avoid being seen by the Butcher Gang.)

AGGRESSION: Bathe in violence. (Don't die during the battle in the Lost Harbor.)

NO NEED FOR A SPOON: Collect all the Bacon Soup in Chapter 5 (see page 140).

 TOE TAPPIN': Turn on the radio in Chapter 5. (When you enter the second room in the Film Vault, open the box on the floor directly to your left. The radio is inside it.)

 NOW HEAR THIS!: Listen to all audio logs in Chapter 5 (see page 141).

 STANDING PROUD: Find out where you belong. (After completing the game, a new Archives chapter will unlock. In the chapter, there is a pedestal and Henry Stein's biography on a sign next to it. Jump onto the pedestal to earn this achievement.)

 A SWEET DISCOVERY: Say hello to an old friend. (After finishing the pipe puzzle, return to the Administration offices. As you approach the office of Joey Drew, turn down the hall to your left. The first door on the right opens onto an office containing a "Sheep Songs" poster. Walk through that wall to visit theMeatly.)

ULTIMATE OVERACHIEVER

If you've been keeping up with your achievements for each chapter thus far, you'll also earn the following:

 THE VOICE COLLECTOR: Listen to all audio logs in the game.

 GOLD RECORD: Turn on all of the hidden radios in the game.

 MASTER OF BACON: Collect all of the Bacon Soup in the game.

 GRAND PUPPETEER: Find theMeatly in all chapters.

STUDIO LAYOUT

NO NEED FOR A SPOON

There are seven cans of Bacon Soup scattered throughout the studio in Chapter 5. Be sure to get them all for the "No Need for a Spoon" achievement.

- Four cans, in the hideout, three on the shelf to the left as you break out of your prison; one can around the corner on your left, under a cot against the wall.

- One can, in Administration, on a chair to the right of the office of Joey Drew.

- Two cans, in Administration, on a shelf in the closet across from the office of Joey Drew.

BRIAR LABEL
BACON SOUP

NOW HEAR THIS!

You'll need to listen to all the audio logs in this chapter for the "Still Listening" achievement:

- Thomas Connor, Administration lobby; head through the doors to the pipe puzzle, then turn right into the office alcove.
- Joey Drew, Administration offices; enter Administration and enter the door at the end of the first hallway.
- Wally Franks, Administration offices; enter Administration and turn right at the end of the first hallway. Enter the office on your right.
- Joey Drew, Administration offices; enter Administration and turn right at the end of the hallway. Round the left corner and enter the office on your right. Turning left, you'll find this audio log on a table between two locked doors, under a "Gent" sign.
- Joey Drew, Administration offices; enter the office of Joey Drew.

CASH

THE SCYTHE

An incredibly powerful weapon is accessible in Chapter 5, provided you've played through the game up to this point having accomplished the following:

- Start the game from Chapter 1 and make it to the Administration offices in Chapter 5 without dying.
- In Chapter 2, crush the Miner Searcher where you crushed Swollen Jack (see page 42).
- In Chapter 3, defeat the Searcher Boss in the Lever Challenge (see page 71).
- In Chapter 4, defeat the Butcher Gang, Bertrum Piedmont, the Projectionist, and Brute Boris with the thirty-one empty Bacon Soup cans you found in Research & Development (see page 109).
- Solve the pipe puzzle to drain the Film Vault entrance and open the door, but do not head inside yet.
- Return to the Administration offices and locate a large open room in which the far wall has been removed. In the rubble, you'll find the Scythe.

- Picking it up will cause Searchers to spawn. Proceed to the office of Joey Drew, where a Searcher wearing Sammy Lawrence's mask will spawn. Defeat it and finish Chapter 5 without dying.

- Continue into your restart of Chapter 1. Proceed downstairs into the area where you found *The Illusion of Living* book. In the previously blocked-off hallway past the tables, the passage will now be clear. Descend through the trapdoor and down more stairs to find an inky tunnel, one that looks eerily similar to the death screen.

- Going through the tunnel will lead you back to the beginning of the chapter. A strange filter will appear over the screen, looking like an old cel-shaded cartoon.

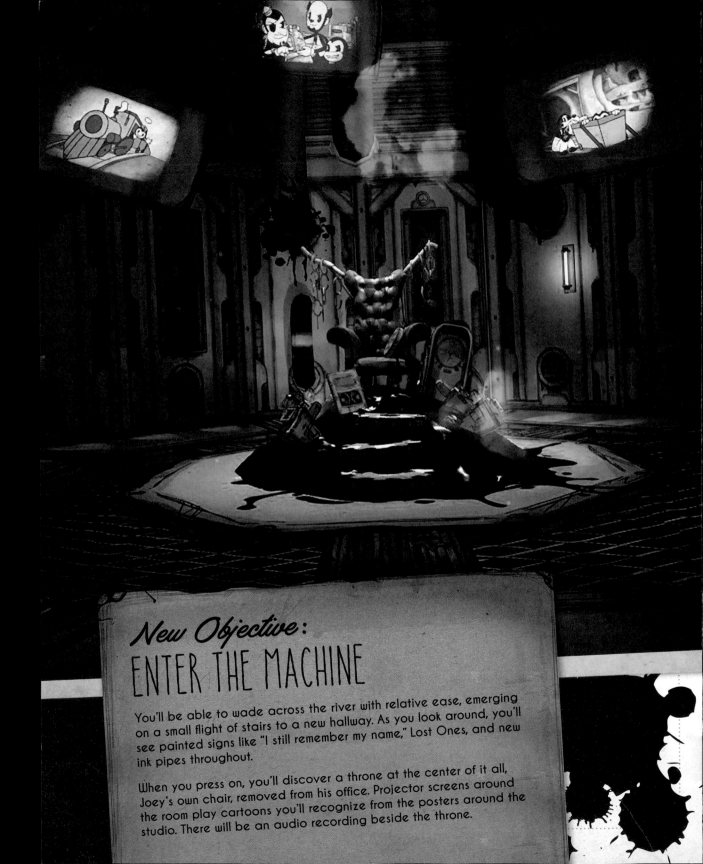

New Objective:
ENTER THE MACHINE

You'll be able to wade across the river with relative ease, emerging on a small flight of stairs to a new hallway. As you look around, you'll see painted signs like "I still remember my name," Lost Ones, and new ink pipes throughout.

When you press on, you'll discover a throne at the center of it all, Joey's own chair, removed from his office. Projector screens around the room play cartoons you'll recognize from the posters around the studio. There will be an audio recording beside the throne.

IT'S SIMPLY AWE—INSPIRING WHAT ONE CAN ACCOMPLISH WITH THEIR OWN HANDS.

A LUMP OF CLAY CAN TURN TO MEANING... IF YOU STRANGLE IT WITH ENOUGH ENTHUSIASM. LOOK WHAT WE'VE BUILT. WE CREATED LIFE ITSELF, HENRY! NOT JUST ON THE SILVER SCREEN, BUT IN THE HEARTS OF THOSE WE ENTERTAINED WITH OUR FANCY MOVING PICTURES. BUT... WHEN THE TICKETS STOPPED SELLING... WHEN THE NEXT BIG THING CAME ALONG... ONLY THE MONSTERS REMAINED... SHADOWS OF THE PAST. BUT YOU CAN SAVE THEM, HENRY! YOU CAN PEEL IT ALL AWAY! YOU SEE,

THERE'S ONLY ONE THING BENDY HAS NEVER KNOWN. HE WAS THERE FOR HIS BEGINNING... BUT HE'S NEVER SEEN: THE END.

BEAST BENDY

After the audio recording is complete, you'll see Ink Bendy appear behind the throne. As you watch, Ink Bendy mutates again into Beast Bendy, with atrophied legs, massive claws, and a sharp-toothed smile. You'll need to tread carefully in this final battle—any hit from Bendy brings instant death.

PHASE 1

Escape into a large open maze of hallways. Beast Bendy will run down each corridor, disappearing into the walls. You'll need to dodge, hide, and run from him while you locate four power switches. Flipping these will open a door to a new area.

Tip: Use the Seeing Tool to reveal arrows that will lead you to a path that is best suited for finding the power switches.

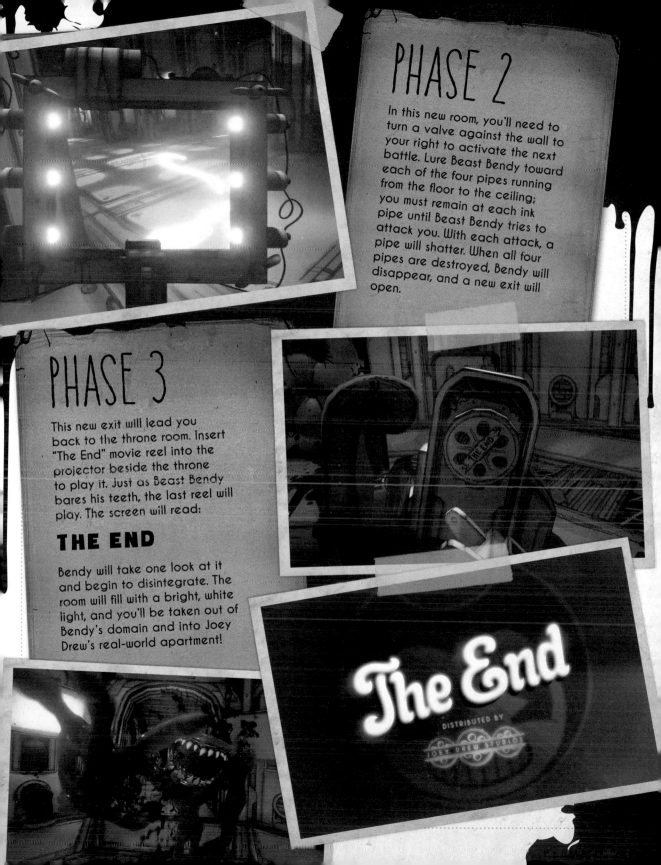

PHASE 2

In this new room, you'll need to turn a valve against the wall to your right to activate the next battle. Lure Beast Bendy toward each of the four pipes running from the floor to the ceiling; you must remain at each ink pipe until Beast Bendy tries to attack you. With each attack, a pipe will shatter. When all four pipes are destroyed, Bendy will disappear, and a new exit will open.

PHASE 3

This new exit will lead you back to the throne room. Insert "The End" movie reel into the projector beside the throne to play it. Just as Beast Bendy bares his teeth, the last reel will play. The screen will read:

THE END

Bendy will take one look at it and begin to disintegrate. The room will fill with a bright, white light, and you'll be taken out of Bendy's domain and into Joey Drew's real-world apartment!

Dear Mr. Drew,

I have to say it was a big surprise getting a letter from you after all these years! I'm surprised you even remember me from back in the old days at the studio. I mostly just swept up the place.

I'm good here in Florida, lots of sun for me and the Mrs. Hope you're doing very good, too.

Sorry to hear about the studio closing down. You all made some great little cartoons there. They was good for some laughs!

Ok, I gotta wrap this up. The grandkids want to hit the beach, so I'm outta here!

 — Wally Franks

Joey,

Sorry it's been quite a while since my last letter. Been busy with work at Archgate Films. The studio ordered another sequel! So I have been spending many hours in the recording booth again! It's fun though.

Tom is doing good, thanks for asking. He's always tinkering on something. Mostly he's still upset about someone stealing one of his dusty inventions from your old studio. He'll get over it.

Have a good New Year, Joey. I'll send you another recipe soon.

Warm regards,
Allison Connor

TITLE: "BENDY & THE INK MACHINE"
sketches & concepts

shotgun?

Alt

Medium

125

flicker

pan-left

long shot

JD

Page 47.

TITLE: "BENDY & THE INK MACHINE"
sketches & concepts

ym

Bendy wins.

B.

JD

JOEY DREW'S APARTMENT

Take your time to explore Joey Drew's apartment. On a shelf to the right of the door you entered through, you'll notice all the objects you placed on pedestals in Chapter 1. A bulletin board to the left of the kitchen doorway contains letters from former employees of the studio, unpaid bills, a notice of bankruptcy, a photograph, and a colored concept sketch of Bendyland. To the right of the kitchen doorway, Joey's drawing table is littered with storyboard panels from different story beats of Chapters 1–5.

Continuing into the kitchen, you'll find Joey himself standing at the kitchen sink, washing dishes and whistling Bendy's song. He'll acknowledge that you have questions. Then he'll say that he has a question of his own: "Who are we, Henry?" Joey will continue.

"IN THE END, WE FOLLOWED TWO DIFFERENT ROADS OF OUR OWN MAKING. YOU, A LOVELY FAMILY... ME... A CROOKED EMPIRE. AND MY ROAD BURNED. I LET OUR CREATIONS BECOME MY LIFE. THE TRUTH IS, YOU WERE ALWAYS SO GOOD AT PUSHING, OLD FRIEND... PUSHING ME TO DO THE RIGHT THING. YOU SHOULD HAVE PUSHED A LITTLE HARDER. HENRY, COME VISIT THE OLD WORKSHOP. THERE'S SOMETHING I WANT TO SHOW YOU."

The calendar date on the wall in the kitchen changes with each playthrough.

Through the door in Joey's apartment, you'll be led back to the beginning of the workshop. After the credits roll, a bonus scene will play. From the kitchen, the camera pans to the opposite wall, where a picture of Bendy, Boris, and Alice hangs. You'll be able to catch a glimpse of Joey's garage through the doorway, which contains the infamous Ink Machine. As you zoom in on the picture, a little girl's voice says, "Tell me another one, Uncle Joey."

Congratulations on your success!
Your Best Pal,
Henry Stein

After completing the game, you'll be able to unlock the Seeing Tool in all chapters, as well as bonus content, a new chapter called *The Archives*.

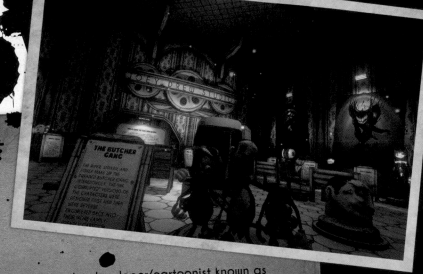

Bonus Content:
WELCOME TO THE ARCHIVES

Bendy and the Ink Machine began when the developer/cartoonist known as theMeatly experimented with bringing a sketched 2-D style into a 3-D world. After turning the idea into a horror game, Chapter 1 of the game was created in a little under a week with a programmer/friend, Mike Mood, and released on February 10, 2017. Much to their surprise, it struck a chord with global indie gamers almost overnight. TheMeatly and Mike Mood decided to drop all other projects to work on Bendy and tell a most unique ink story.

The entire game was completed a chapter at a time in a year and a half by a small but dedicated group of indie developers. Although the concept and story remained as originally intended, the game changed over development as characters and models were refined from their early "thrown-together" versions. This archive is a peek behind the scenes at that process.

Hop up onto the empty pedestal to unlock the "Standing Proud" achievement!

HENRY STEIN

ONCE AN EQUAL BUSINESS PARTNER OF JOEY DREW, HENRY STEIN WAS A TALENTED ANIMATOR AND CHARACTER DESIGNER UNTIL LEAVING THE COMPANY AROUND 1930. HIS PLACE IN JOEY DREW STUDIOS' HISTORY IS SOMEWHAT UNDOCUMENTED, BUT HE IS OFTEN RUMORED TO BE THE TRUE CREATOR BEHIND MANY OF THE STUDIO'S MOST MEMORABLE CHARACTERS.

BETA SEARCHER

EARLY IN DEVELOPMENT, WITH JUST A FEW WEEKS TO CREATE CHAPTER 2, THE BETA SEARCHERS WERE DESIGNED IN RECORD TIME BEFORE BEING FULLY RETOOLED LATER ON. THEY WERE THE FIRST FIGHTING ENEMIES ENCOUNTERED IN THE GAME.

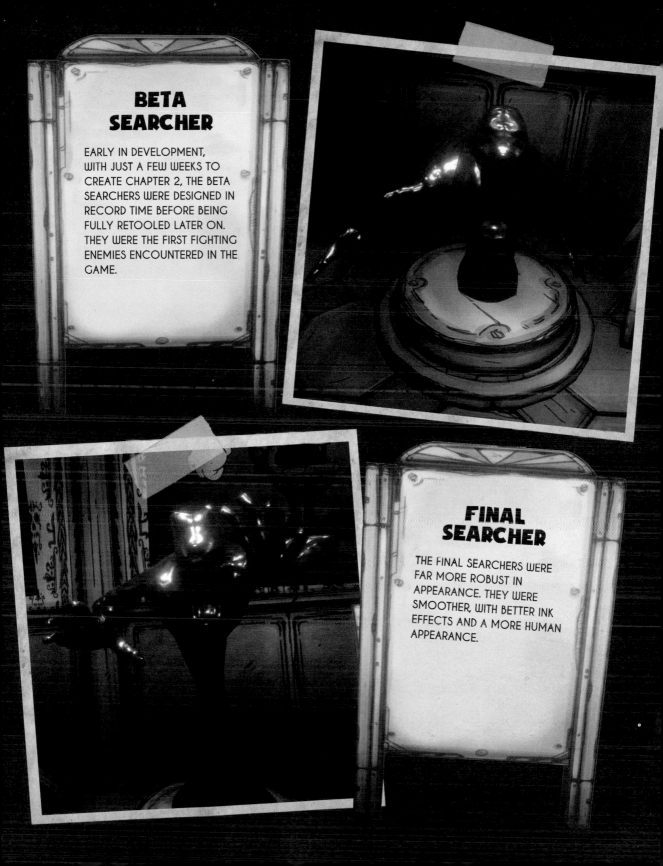

FINAL SEARCHER

THE FINAL SEARCHERS WERE FAR MORE ROBUST IN APPEARANCE. THEY WERE SMOOTHER, WITH BETTER INK EFFECTS AND A MORE HUMAN APPEARANCE.

CONCEPT BENDY

THIS IS THE FIRST VERSION OF BENDY EVER MODELED. IN THE EARLIEST CONCEPTS BENDY WAS MUCH SMALLER (AND CUTER) WITH A FACE THAT SPLIT OPEN TO REVEAL A TERRIFYING MOUTH.

ALPHA BENDY

THIS IS THE ORIGINAL GAME-USED DESIGN OF INK BENDY FROM THE EARLIEST VERSION OF CHAPTER 1. IT IS JOKINGLY REFERRED TO AS "BIRD POOP WITH A SMILE" AMONG THE DEVELOPMENT TEAM.

BETA BENDY

THIS WAS INK BENDY'S FORM UNTIL THE RELEASE OF CHAPTER 4. AT THAT TIME THE GAME RECEIVED A MAJOR VISUAL UPGRADE AND THE TITLE CHARACTER GOT A NEW MODEL AS WELL.

INK BENDY

INK BENDY AS WE KNOW HIM TODAY. ALTHOUGH SIMILAR TO BETA BENDY, THIS UPGRADED VERSION WAS REMODELED, ENHANCED WITH A HIGHER POLYGON COUNT, AND GIVEN NEW INK EFFECTS.

BEAST BENDY

INK BENDY'S HORRIFIC FINAL FORM IN CHAPTER 5 PULLED AWAY THE CARTOON FAÇADE AND REVEALED THE DEMON WITHIN.

BETA SAMMY

WITH HIS FIRST APPEARANCE IN CHAPTER 2, FAN FAVORITE SAMMY LAWRENCE BECAME A TERRIFYINGLY ENTERTAINING CHARACTER. WHEN HIS SLIM BUILD WAS DEEMED NOT THREATENING ENOUGH, HE WAS REDESIGNED AND GIVEN A BETTER SKELETAL RIG FOR MORE ADVANCED ANIMATION.

FINAL SAMMY

SAMMY LAWRENCE'S FINAL FORM CAME COMPLETE WITH A BULKED-UP STATURE AND MORE POWERFUL LIMBS. THE MAD SONGWRITER MAY FINALLY GET NOTICED NOW, AT LEAST BY FANS.

BETA BORIS

"PAPA" WAS THE ORIGINAL NAME OF THE CHARACTER THAT EVENTUALLY BECAME BORIS THE WOLF. THIS EARLY VERSION WAS RELEASED WITH CHAPTER 1. HE WAS QUICKLY REFINED INTO THE BORIS WE KNOW TODAY WITH THE RELEASE OF CHAPTER 2.

BORIS THE WOLF

BORIS THE WOLF, A FRIEND TO THE END, WAS DESIGNED USING VARIOUS REFERENCES FROM CARTOONS OF THE 1920S. A BLEND OF WEST COAST AND EAST COAST ANIMATION STYLES, THIS SILENT AND SUPPORTIVE WOLF WON OVER THE HEARTS OF MANY, ALTHOUGH AT TIMES HE WAS A HEADACHE FOR THE DEVELOPMENT TEAM DUE TO HIS AI TAKING ON A MIND OF ITS OWN DURING PRODUCTION.

BRUTE BORIS

ALICE ANGEL'S MONSTROSITY, BRUTE BORIS, WAS ONE OF THE BIGGEST SURPRISES OF CHAPTER 4. HIS DESIGN WAS ROUGHLY BASED ON FRANKENSTEIN'S MONSTER BUT WITH A MORE UNFINISHED APPEARANCE. ALICE TOOK PARTS FROM WITHIN HIM AND SUBSTITUTED THINGS THAT HIS BODY IS RAPIDLY REJECTING.

ORIGINAL INK MACHINE

BEFORE A MAJOR VISUAL UPGRADE, THIS VERSION OF THE INK MACHINE WAS THE ONE USED IN THE GAME. MUCH OF THIS MACHINE'S ICONIC, FAN-LOVED DESIGN WAS TRANSLATED INTO THE FINAL VERSION.

THE BUTCHER GANG

THE PIPER, STRIKER, AND FISHER MAKE UP THE DREADED BUTCHER GANG. INTERESTINGLY, THE "INK-CORRUPTED" VERSIONS OF THE CHARACTERS WERE DESIGNED FIRST AND THEN WERE REVERSE ENGINEERED BACK INTO THEIR MORE FAMILY-FRIENDLY CARTOON FORMS.

STRIKERS

PIPERS

FISHERS

LIAR

BERTRUM
PIEDMONT
HEAD

TWISTED
ALICE

ALICE

SECRET MESSAGES IN CHAPTERS 1–4

Once you've completed the main story, you'll unlock the Seeing Tool to use in Chapters 1–4. Hundreds of secret messages exist in these chapters, but some of the best appear below.

- Chapter 1, entrance hallway: Tally marks line the walls.

- Chapter 1, Henry's desktop: "He was born here."

- Chapter 1, toilet in the Animation Department: "Can I get a little privacy?"

- Chapter 1, floor in front of the Ink Machine: "There *never* was a choice."

- Chapter 1, in front of the sacrificed Boris: "She's heartless."

- Chapter 1, radio room: "Listening and always watching"

- Chapter 1, theMeatly's room: "Devilishly handsome"

- Chapter 1, room after the fall, where you get the axe: "Joey lied to us."

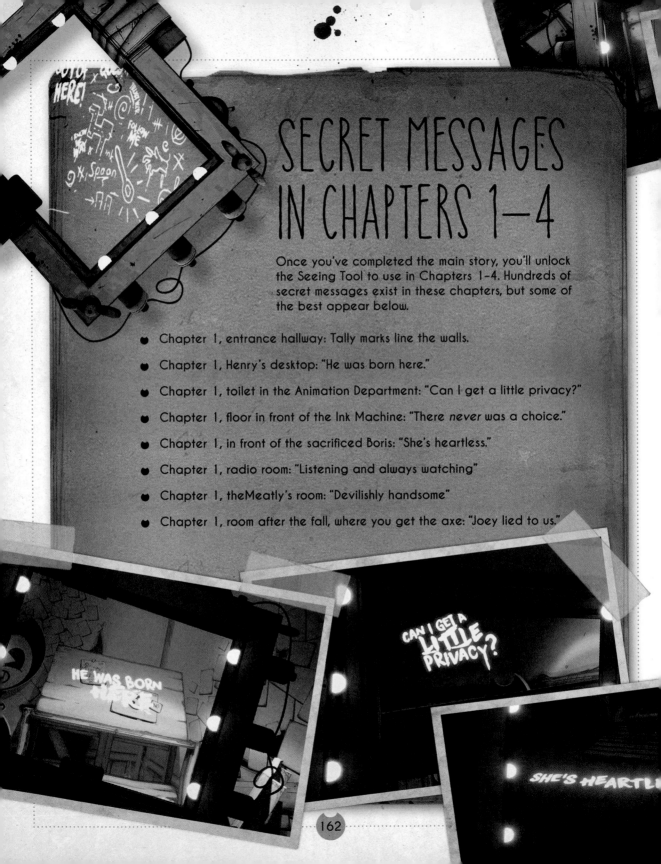

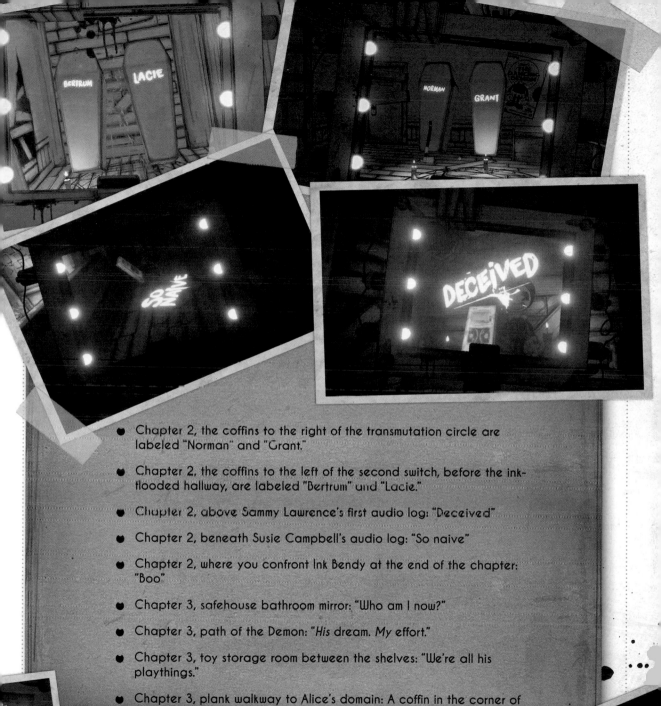

- Chapter 2, the coffins to the right of the transmutation circle are labeled "Norman" and "Grant."

- Chapter 2, the coffins to the left of the second switch, before the ink-flooded hallway, are labeled "Bertrum" and "Lacie."

- Chapter 2, above Sammy Lawrence's first audio log: "Deceived"

- Chapter 2, beneath Susie Campbell's audio log: "So naive"

- Chapter 2, where you confront Ink Bendy at the end of the chapter: "Boo"

- Chapter 3, safehouse bathroom mirror: "Who am I now?"

- Chapter 3, path of the Demon: "*His* dream. *My* effort."

- Chapter 3, toy storage room between the shelves: "We're all his playthings."

- Chapter 3, plank walkway to Alice's domain: A coffin in the corner of the room is labeled "Susie."

- Chapter 3, Alice's room: "Blah blah blah blah"

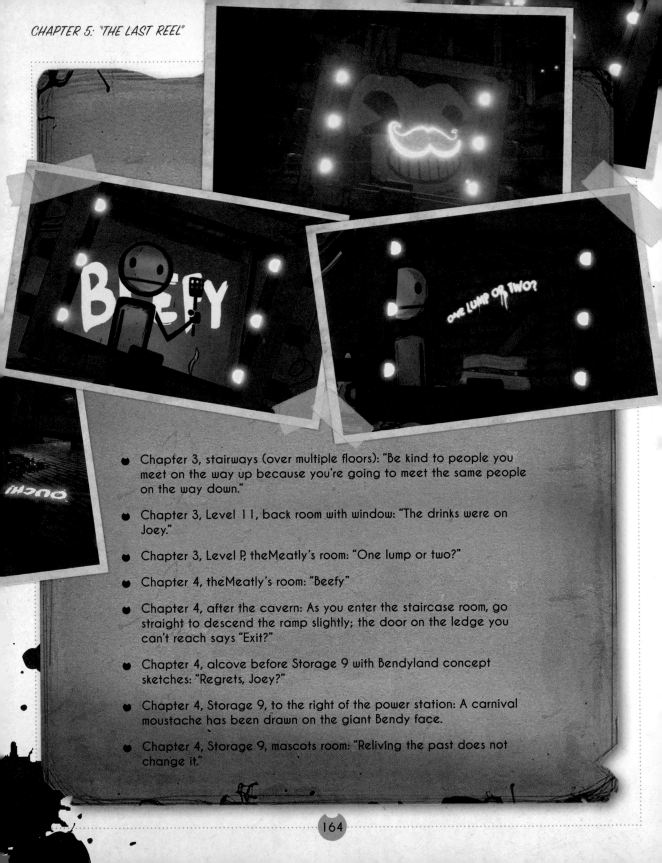

- Chapter 3, stairways (over multiple floors): "Be kind to people you meet on the way up because you're going to meet the same people on the way down."

- Chapter 3, Level 11, back room with window: "The drinks were on Joey."

- Chapter 3, Level P, theMeatly's room: "One lump or two?"

- Chapter 4, theMeatly's room: "Beefy"

- Chapter 4, after the cavern: As you enter the staircase room, go straight to descend the ramp slightly; the door on the ledge you can't reach says "Exit?"

- Chapter 4, alcove before Storage 9 with Bendyland concept sketches: "Regrets, Joey?"

- Chapter 4, Storage 9, to the right of the power station: A carnival moustache has been drawn on the giant Bendy face.

- Chapter 4, Storage 9, mascots room: "Reliving the past does not change it."

- Chapter 4, Research & Design, under the Lost One's cage: "Please don't cry."

- Chapter 4, Research & Design, on the box beside the animatronic: "It never moves."

- Chapter 4, Attractions, Bertrum Piedmont's room, under the "Buddy Boris Railway" poster: "Time wounds all heels."

- Chapter 4, Maintenance, first floor beside Joey's audio log: "That's the Joey I knew."

- Chapter 5, Henry's prison in the hideout: The notes above Henry's cot include three notes in a different handwriting style ("ink," "spoon," "escape"). Who left these?

- Chapter 5, office of Joey Drew, above the door: "Who is the man behind the monster?"

- Chapter 5, after Tom and Alice rejoin you in the Film Vault, look through your viewfinder at Tom; if you gave Boris a bone in Chapter 3, a bone will be visible in Tom's mouth here.

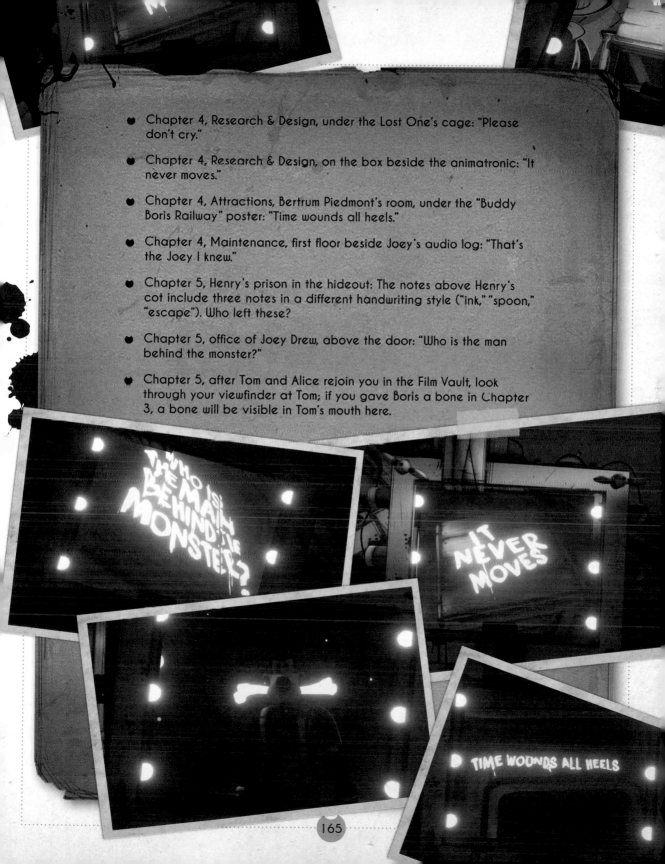

PART II

WELCOME TO THE STUDIO!

Now that you've gotten through your first week, it's time to take a closer look at Joey Drew Studios. In this section, you'll learn about the company's employee benefits as well as incentives, rewards, and organizational charts.

Mister Drew,

I'm happy to share our top-secret Briar Label Bacon Soup recipe with you! Please be sure to keep this somewhere safe though. We'd be ruined if our competitors found out there's no beef in the soup.

– Wilfred Briar

BRIAR LABEL BACON SOUP

INGREDIENTS

- 1 lb. premium Canadian bacon
- ¾ cup chopped onion
- ¾ cup peeled, diced carrots
- ¾ cup diced celery
- 4 cups peeled, diced potatoes
- 4 tbsps butter
- 3 cups chicken broth
- ¼ cup flour
- 2 cups cheddar cheese
- 1 cup milk
- ½ cup heavy cream
- 1 tsp salt
- 1 tsp pepper

Kids, ask an adult to help you!

INSTRUCTIONS

1. Using 1 tbsp of butter, sauté onions, carrots, and celery in a large soup pot until tender. Add chopped bacon to the pot and cook until crispy.

2. Add broth and potatoes to your soup pot, bringing it to a boil. Reduce heat, keeping the soup on a simmer. Cook ten minutes, or until potatoes are tender.

3. Combine 3 tbsps of butter with the flour in a skillet, cooking for roughly five minutes, or until bubbly. Add this to the soup pot, and bring it to a boil once again. Reduce heat, simmering soup for another 3-5 minutes.

4. Reduce heat to low. Stir heavy cream, milk, cheese, salt, and pepper into the soup pot, cooking until cheese is melted.

ANIMATION DEPARTMENT ORGANIZATIONAL CHART

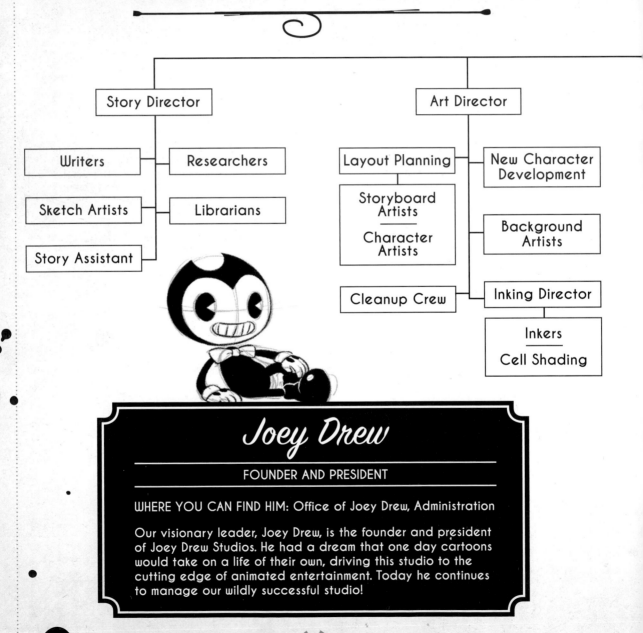

- Story Director
  - Writers
  - Researchers
  - Sketch Artists
  - Librarians
  - Story Assistant

- Art Director
  - Layout Planning
  - New Character Development
  - Storyboard Artists
  - Character Artists
  - Background Artists
  - Cleanup Crew
  - Inking Director
  - Inkers
  - Cell Shading

Joey Drew

FOUNDER AND PRESIDENT

WHERE YOU CAN FIND HIM: Office of Joey Drew, Administration

Our visionary leader, Joey Drew, is the founder and president of Joey Drew Studios. He had a dream that one day cartoons would take on a life of their own, driving this studio to the cutting edge of animated entertainment. Today he continues to manage our wildly successful studio!

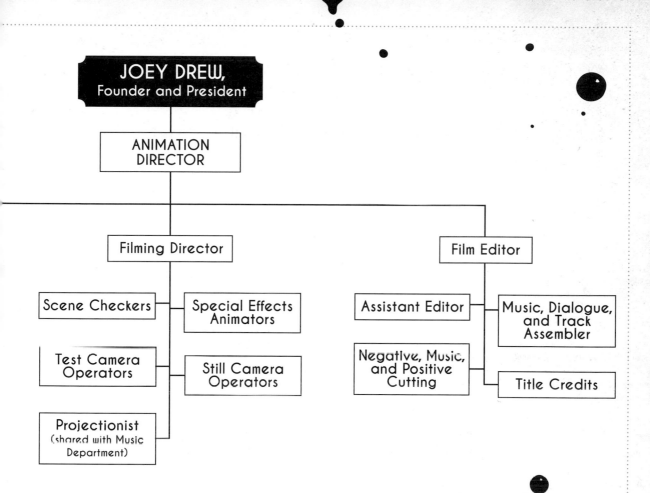

JOEY DREW,
Founder and President

ANIMATION DIRECTOR

Filming Director

Scene Checkers

Special Effects Animators

Test Camera Operators

Still Camera Operators

Projectionist
(shared with Music Department)

Film Editor

Assistant Editor

Music, Dialogue, and Track Assembler

Negative, Music, and Positive Cutting

Title Credits

Norman Polk

PROJECTIONIST

WHERE YOU CAN FIND HIM: Anywhere!

Norman is the cinematic expert at Joey Drew Studios. A bit of a recluse, Norman much prefers the quiet of the theater to the hubbub of the bull pen, but he's happy to help with any questions you may have, should you manage to find him.

Welcome to the Animation Department!

RESTROOM: To your left you will find the restrooms. This is important to note, as you'll be spending a lot of time in the Animation Department and will need to use the toilet probably no more than once a day. We'd explain more, but surely you know how to use the bathroom, yes?

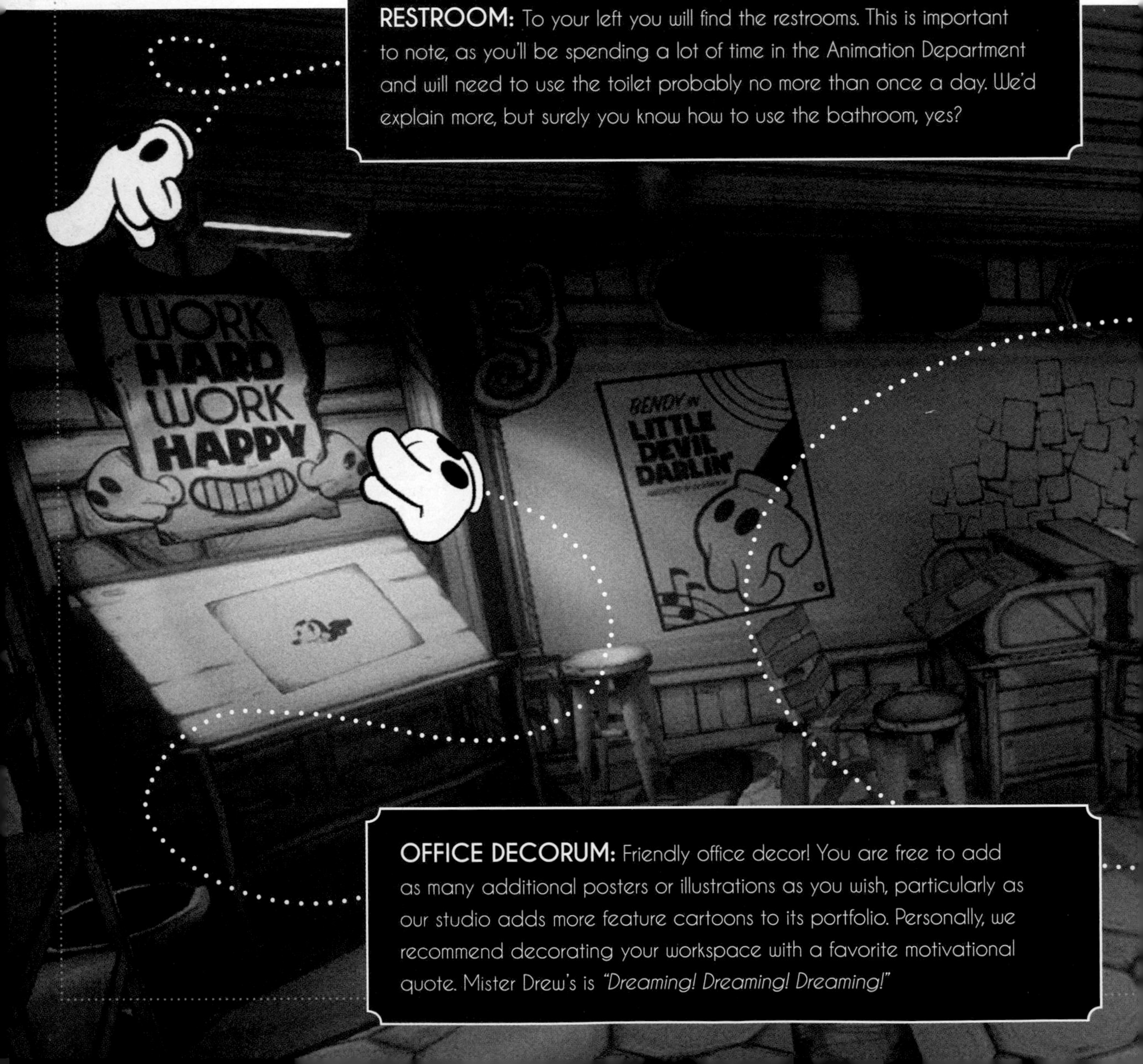

WORK
HARD
WORK
HAPPY

BENDY IN
LITTLE
DEVIL
DARLIN'

OFFICE DECORUM: Friendly office decor! You are free to add as many additional posters or illustrations as you wish, particularly as our studio adds more feature cartoons to its portfolio. Personally, we recommend decorating your workspace with a favorite motivational quote. Mister Drew's is *"Dreaming! Dreaming! Dreaming!"*

Down a small flight of stairs you will find the Animation Department, home to all our hardworking storyboard artists, concept artists, pencilers, inkers, and animators. It is here where the magic of animation is brought to life! This is one of the newer rooms at Joey Drew Studios, expanded to fit our rapidly growing staff. It has been modernized and updated with our artists' comfort in mind. Take a peek: This is the place where dreams are born!

BENDY: Aha! Your eyes went straight to Bendy! They say a creator shouldn't pick favorites, but Bendy is by far our most beloved character here at Joey Drew Studios. He can be seen in all of our greatest animated shorts, and his wonderful grin will be much like yours once you start delving into your new role here. Feel free to shake Bendy's cardboard hand for luck—not that you'll need it, of course.

ANIMATORS AT WORK: Here is where our animators sit. If you are an animator joining our team, welcome! Their high-technology drawing boards are lighted from below to ensure each cel matches its partners as closely as possible. And don't these state-of-the-art chairs look extra comfortable? We know our artists will be sitting quite a lot. Nothing inspires dreams quite like hardwood chairs!

MUSIC DEPARTMENT ORGANIZATIONAL CHART

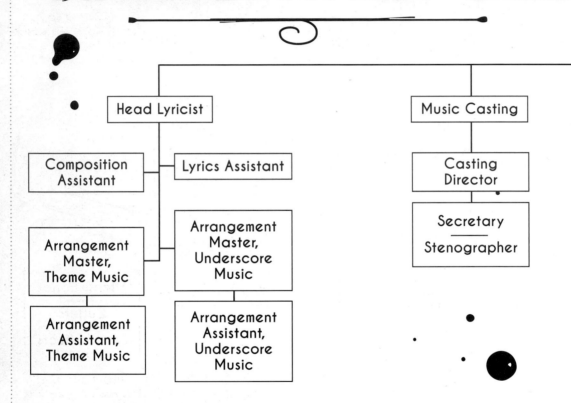

Head Lyricist

Composition Assistant

Lyrics Assistant

Arrangement Master, Theme Music

Arrangement Master, Underscore Music

Arrangement Assistant, Theme Music

Arrangement Assistant, Underscore Music

Music Casting

Casting Director

Secretary
———
Stenographer

Sammy Lawrence
MUSIC DIRECTOR

WHERE YOU CAN FIND HIM: Office of Music Director, Music Department

Sammy Lawrence is the company's music director, responsible for all the audio in our cartoons, including theme songs, scores, voice recordings, and sound effects.

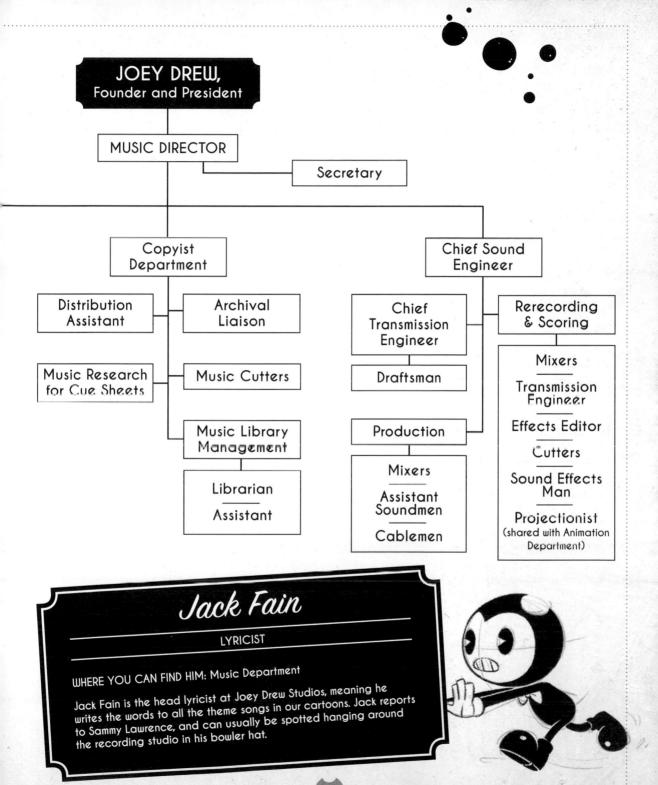

JOEY DREW,
Founder and President

MUSIC DIRECTOR

Secretary

Copyist Department

Distribution Assistant

Archival Liaison

Music Research for Cue Sheets

Music Cutters

Music Library Management

Librarian
—
Assistant

Chief Sound Engineer

Chief Transmission Engineer

Draftsman

Production

Mixers
Assistant Soundmen
Cablemen

Rerecording & Scoring

Mixers
—
Transmission Engineer
Effects Editor
—
Cutters
Sound Effects Man
Projectionist
(shared with Animation Department)

Jack Fain

LYRICIST

WHERE YOU CAN FIND HIM: Music Department

Jack Fain is the head lyricist at Joey Drew Studios, meaning he writes the words to all the theme songs in our cartoons. Jack reports to Sammy Lawrence, and can usually be spotted hanging around the recording studio in his bowler hat.

Welcome to the Music Department!

BAND SEATING: The recording studio is loaded with sheet music stands as well as our state-of-the-art hardwood chairs for comfortable seating. Microphones overhead capture every sound the band makes—from the delicate trilling of a flute to the soft, steady thrums of the bass fiddle.

STORAGE: In here the Music Department stores some of the larger musical instruments it keeps stocked, including bass fiddles and drums.

On Level 3 is our Music Department, where our animated features find their voice. This is one of our modernized recording studios, which features recording booths for our band and voice actors. Here, expert voice talent meets genius musical talent, combining to form a beautiful symphony in lockstep with the animation.

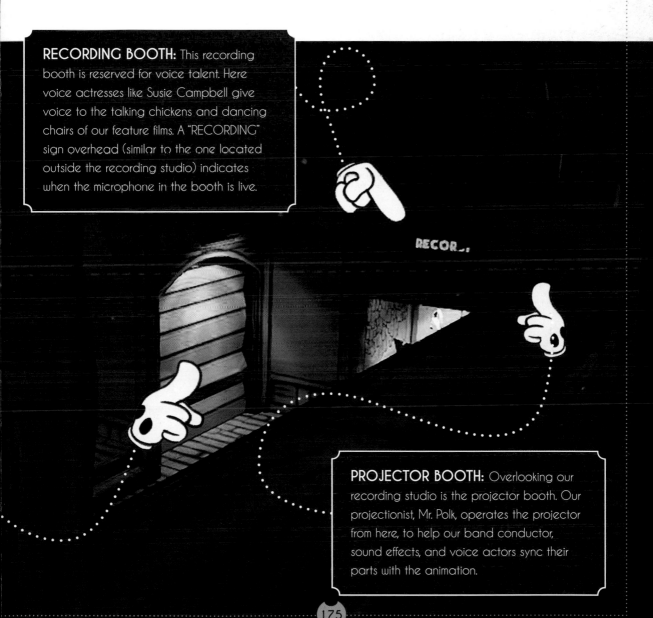

RECORDING BOOTH: This recording booth is reserved for voice talent. Here voice actresses like Susie Campbell give voice to the talking chickens and dancing chairs of our feature films. A "RECORDING" sign overhead (similar to the one located outside the recording studio) indicates when the microphone in the booth is live.

PROJECTOR BOOTH: Overlooking our recording studio is the projector booth. Our projectionist, Mr. Polk, operates the projector from here, to help our band conductor, sound effects, and voice actors sync their parts with the animation.

Accounting & Finance Department
Organizational Chart

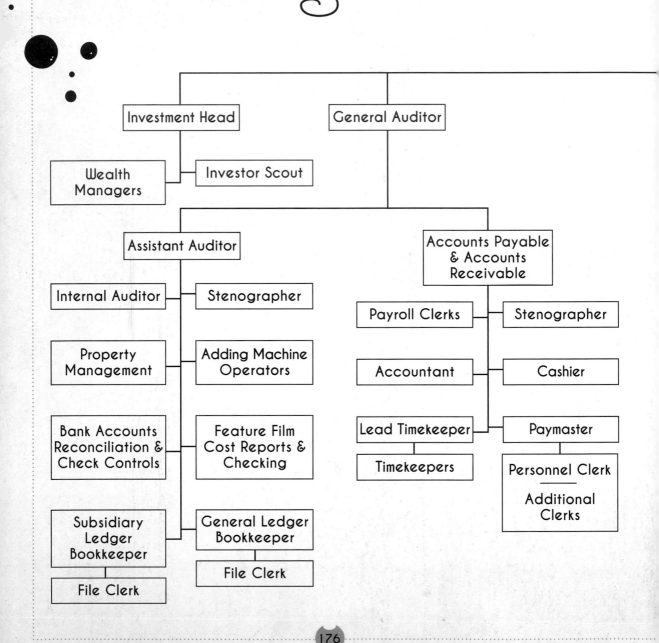

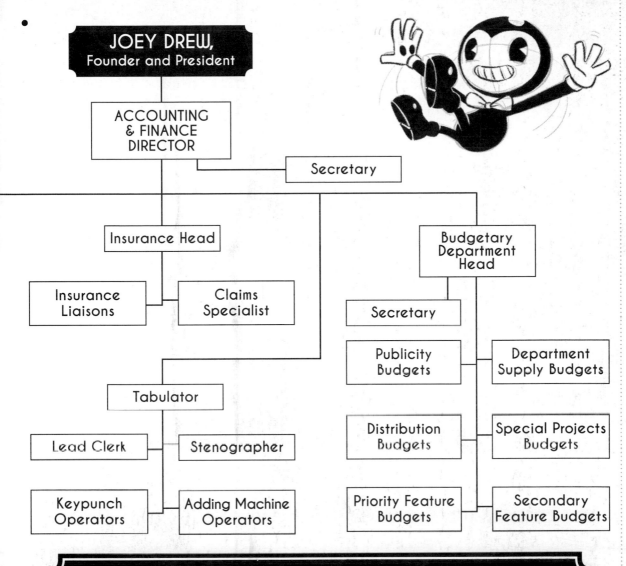

JOEY DREW,
Founder and President

ACCOUNTING & FINANCE DIRECTOR

Secretary

Insurance Head

Insurance Liaisons

Claims Specialist

Budgetary Department Head

Secretary

Publicity Budgets

Department Supply Budgets

Tabulator

Distribution Budgets

Special Projects Budgets

Lead Clerk

Stenographer

Keypunch Operators

Adding Machine Operators

Priority Feature Budgets

Secondary Feature Budgets

Grant Cohen

ACCOUNTING & FINANCE DIRECTOR

WHERE YOU CAN FIND HIM: Accounting & Finance Offices, Level S

Although Grant isn't exactly a creative dreamer, he does dream . . . in numbers. As the Accounting & Finance director, Grant is able to balance the company's checkbooks, funds, and make sure everything is staying afloat. He reports directly to Joey Drew.

ADMINISTRATION AND SPECIAL PROJECTS DEPARTMENTS ORGANIZATIONAL CHART

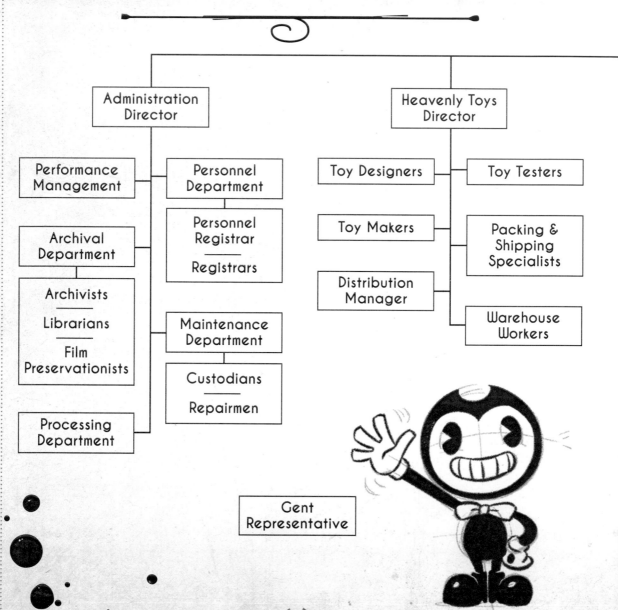

Administration Director

- Performance Management
- Archival Department
  - Archivists
  - Librarians
  - Film Preservationists
- Processing Department

- Personnel Department
  - Personnel Registrar
  - Registrars
- Maintenance Department
  - Custodians
  - Repairmen

Heavenly Toys Director

- Toy Designers
- Toy Makers
- Distribution Manager

- Toy Testers
- Packing & Shipping Specialists
- Warehouse Workers

Gent Representative

JOEY DREW,
Founder and President

Special Projects Director, Bendyland

Lead Engineer

Assistant Engineers, Games

Assistant Engineers, Attractions

Assistant Engineers, Construction

Construction Manager

Warehouse Workers

Assemblers

Machinists

Site Manager

Financial Planner

Materials Specialist

Vendor Liaison

Budget Manager

Shawn Flynn

TOY MAKER

WHERE YOU CAN FIND HIM: Heavenly Toys Room

Shawn Flynn is a toy maker with our subsidiary, Heavenly Toys. He uses our machinery to create toys that feel on brand for Bendy and the other cartoon characters.

Lacie Benton

ENGINEER, SPECIAL PROJECTS, BENDYLAND

WHERE YOU CAN FIND HER: Bendyland Research & Design

Lacie works alongside Special Projects director Bertie Piedmont to help bring the Bendyland dream to life.

Wally Franks

JANITOR

WHERE YOU CAN FIND HIM: Throughout the Studio

Wally is a janitor within our Maintenance Department. In addition to cleaning up general employee messes, Wally's role has recently expanded to assist with malfunctions of Gent machinery.

Thomas Connor

GENT REPRESENTATIVE

WHERE YOU CAN FIND HIM: Throughout the Studio

Thomas Connor is a representative for Gent Corporation, which has produced much of the plumbing and new technology around our studio. He can often be seen milling about the studio, making sure the piping is running as it should. While Thomas isn't strictly an employee of the studio, he is like family to us!

Welcome to the Administration Department!

GENT OFFICE: Our representative from Gent Corporation, Thomas Connor, keeps a satellite office near Administration for the sake of convenience. Our long-standing partnership with Gent, ongoing repair work, and new projects often warrant Gent's urgent attention.

LOBBY SEATING: Our receiving room for those on official business with Administration. Take a seat on one of our many comfortable couches and review paperwork, business proposals, or pitches while you wait for your party to join you.

RECEPTION DESK: Check in with Reception whenever you have a matter that requires an Administration official's attention. Our team of receptionists can page your point of contact.

Your first stop at Joey Drew Studios will very likely be at the Administration offices. This winding labyrinth of corridors and offices is home to the paper pushers who—quite literally—push our company forward each day. You can thank them for processing your new hire paperwork, biweekly paychecks, annual performance evaluations, and more! It might not be the most exciting place to work, but Administration is a vital cog in our company that keeps us up and running.

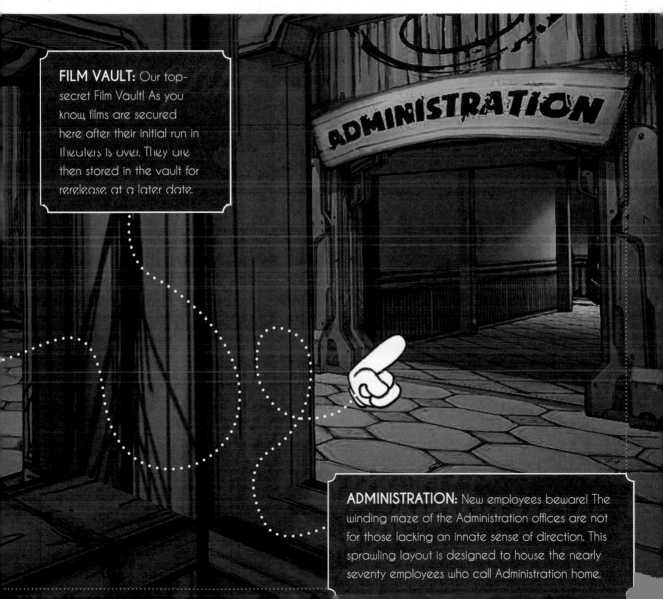

FILM VAULT: Our top-secret Film Vault! As you know, films are secured here after their initial run in theaters is over. They are then stored in the vault for rerelease at a later date.

ADMINISTRATION: New employees beware! The winding maze of the Administration offices are not for those lacking an innate sense of direction. This sprawling layout is designed to house the nearly seventy employees who call Administration home.

What We Expect of You

We hate to invoke the threatening tone of "Rules and Regulations," but we also want to make sure you know what's expected of you and your work for our wonderful company.

Joey Drew Studios hires strictly the best, and that's all we expect of you—the best. Working hours at the studio are set for 8:00 AM to 5:00 PM, but overtime is frequently required to meet our rigorous deadlines. Overtime will be needed after normal studio hours and on weekends during our high-output periods of the year. A reminder that if you are part of our Animation, Music, or Special Projects Departments, you are likely salaried and thus ineligible for overtime pay. You can avoid unpaid overtime work requirements by completing projects to the highest standards in a timely manner.

Remember: Mister Drew is listening and always watching! Tardiness, personal phone calls, lengthy lunch breaks, and time spent socializing will not go unnoticed and could result in disciplinary action.

We observe a casual dress policy at the studio to foster an atmosphere conducive to creativity, but please keep in mind that business attire may be required for high-level meetings. We ask that you convene with your supervisor if you are unsure of the dress code for a particular event.

Mister Drew built this studio through perseverance and imagination, but also through collaboration and friendship. Poor attitudes, negativity, and gossip distract from our sacred mission to bring joy to the children of the world. Termination will be considered if such behavior becomes prevalent in your work, so be sure to put on a smile at all times!

Your First Day at the Studio

The morning of your first day, please report directly to Administration for new employee processing. Your first morning will be spent navigating the labyrinth of Administration offices, as we set you up in our various systems of record keeping.

First stop: Registration! Our Personnel Registrar will collect Packet 12A from you. As you know, this packet includes information about your position, salary, contact information, and employment history. This packet will start your file at our company, to which will ultimately be added performance evaluations, any merit raises/promotions, and (though we hope not) any disciplinary actions taken against you. At this point, you will also be issued your own identification badge, which you will need to show to reception as you enter and exit the studio.

Next stop: Payroll! Be sure to bring your forms from Packet 524B so Payroll can process your information and set up your paychecks. Here you will also meet the Paymaster. As you might imagine, the Paymaster is responsible for overseeing and delivering your paycheck. Every other Friday is payday, when the Paymaster travels to each department to hand-deliver checks. If you miss the Paymaster during his rounds, you will need to travel to Administration to pick up your paycheck from him directly. Paychecks must be collected in person; delivery to your desk is not permitted.

Finally: Orientation! New Hire Orientation will take you downstairs to the Archives on Level S. Here you'll be treated to a brief history of Joey Drew Studios and our many accomplishments. If you're lucky, Mister Drew himself might even stop by to say hello!

After Orientation, you will be taken to your department and handed over to your supervisor. Take a minute to say hello to your new teammates as they welcome you to the Joey Drew family. Then it's time to get to work!

Health Benefits

Eat some bad bacon? Feel a little nauseated? Come down with a case of . . . well, it's best we don't know. Don't worry, your employer has you covered. Joey Drew Studios is proud to offer a comprehensive health benefits package limited to free, no-charge visits to the studio's state-of-the-art Infirmary. Employees who feel sick need not stay home; simply stop by the Infirmary on your way to your desk. There you'll find a menagerie of treatments and medicines to help you feel better and back to work in no time—no pesky recovery time required! Qualified medical staff are on-site several days each month to consult with you about your needs.

In the unlikely event that you should require sick leave, you may petition for paid sick leave benefits by checking in with Administration. There you can pick up Packets 259B, 1027A, 40L, and 723D. Fill out these forms in triplicate and be sure to submit them to Administration along with a detailed letter from your doctor within two days of absence. If your forms are approved, your pay will be included in your next paycheck.

Besides your health, we also want to make sure you're doing what you can to protect your safety on the job. Be sure to hold the handrails as you ascend and descend the stairways, follow all posted protocols for interacting with equipment, and report any unsafe working conditions to our janitor, Wally Franks. Should an accident occur on the job, please file a report with Administration within twenty-four hours. From there, the condition and any necessary medical leave can be addressed.

We know that, above all else, your heart is in the work we do here. Excessive absences don't benefit yourself or your fellow employees, who still have to complete your department's collective work on time. For this reason, employees are only eligible for five days of paid leave per year. Absences above that number—due to illness or otherwise—will likely result in immediate termination.

Holidays and Vacation Time

Dreams don't happen at random. They come from cultured, happy employees!

To this end, we are thrilled to offer the following holidays off for our employees, noting of course that service the day before and after the holiday is expected: New Year's Day, Memorial Day, July Fourth, Labor Day, Thanksgiving, Christmas.

In some animation studios we will not name, employees are given *paid* vacation time, and while that all sounds fine and dandy, we must ask: Why, in Bendy's good name, would anyone need to take a vacation from their job unless they *hated* it?

Once your company loyalty is proven with five years of continuous service, Joey Drew Studios is thrilled to offer five days of unpaid vacation time, with which we hope you'll take your family on a wholesome, well-earned trip to our Bendyland amusement park when it's complete. We hope these days away from your job give you time to really appreciate it and the inherent value in a hard day's work.

Until you've built up this trust with the company, take a look at some of our wonderful "studio vacations" below. If you catch yourself dreaming of faraway vistas, consider one of these more practical alternatives!

- When you're thinking about Bora Bora . . . Draw your own beach, and hang it up right at your workspace. A big inspiration for "The Dancing Demon" came from our animators dreaming of Hawaii!

- When you're thinking about Mexico . . . Let Mr. Franks tell you about the time he thought he ate some tasty churros but they turned out to be . . . well, we'll let him tell you.

- When you're thinking about Paris . . . Joey Drew currently holds the office record for highest tower of Bacon Soup cans. Can you beat him? Try your best, and don't forget to dispose of your cans in the salvage bin to help with the war effort!

- When you're dreaming about Miami . . . Isn't Florida under sea level? You can be too—just bust off one of the valves in Utility Shaft 9! (This is office humor. You really shouldn't do this, as it's very disruptive.)

Employee Rewards

There are many additional employee rewards available to you while working at Joey Drew Studios. Find out all our animation studio has to offer below!

EMPLOYEE OF THE MONTH

This is a new initiative that we'll be starting soon: Employee of the Month. How it works is simple. Joey Drew was the first employee, so he'll be the first employee of the month. If anyone is better than him, they get to be employee of the month. So far no one's usurped Joey . . . but maybe that will change with you!

FREE TOILET PAPER

Worried you'd have to bring your own toilet paper to the studio? Think again! The bathrooms at Joey Drew Studios are stocked with all the TP your little heart could ever desire. And it's two-ply too. Now that's love! Just don't use too much. Mr. Franks has enough to do.

HOLIDAY BONUSES

The holidays are time for family . . . and when you're here, you're part of Joey's family. To thank you for all of your hard work, we are pleased to reward our employees the opportunity to earn overtime by working Christmas, so you can celebrate our work with the ones you love most—Bendy, Boris the Wolf, and Alice Angel!

HOLIDAY PARTIES

In addition to our Halloween party (which has spooky stories, candied bacon, and a costume contest), we also have various parties throughout the year. We celebrate Bendy's birthday (the day Bendy was created—there's devil's food cake!), Alice Angel's birthday (angel food cake!), Boris's birthday (bacon! Mm, salty), and, of course, Joey Drew's birthday (everyone stays overtime to wish Joey a happy birthday!).

Bendyland

Amusement parks are all the craze these days. It seems like they're everywhere! Fortunately, Bendy fans will have only one themed amusement park to visit from now on—Bendyland. Joey Drew had the fashionable idea at dinner one day, and the endeavor was launched in 1940 with the help of famed amusement park designer Bertrum Piedmont. Mr. Piedmont was hired immediately after Joey had the idea, bringing with him an impressive resume cobbled together from forty years designing parks for various clients.

Bendyland will be home to a number of fantastical and wonderful Bendy-themed attractions, including Light Land, Big Land, Dark Land, and Tiny Land.

Employees of Joey Drew Studios will soon get to reap all the wonderful benefits of Bendyland. In addition to a free lifetime pass* (well, as long as you stay employed here, but that'll be a lifetime!), you also get up to four guest passes, should you somehow mingle with people who aren't your direct coworkers. You'll also get a 40 percent discount to use on your purchases.**

We're thrilled to share more information about Bendyland with you in the coming months!

* The Bendyland Employee Pass is not valid on New Year's Day, Groundhog Day, Mardi Gras, Ash Wednesday, Valentine's Day, Chinese New Year, Purim, Holi, St. Patrick's Day, Good Friday, Easter Sunday, Easter Monday, Passover, Tax Day, Cinco de Mayo, Mother's Day, Ramadan, Memorial Day, Flag Day, Father's Day, Eid al-Fitr, Independence Day, Labor Day, Rosh Hashanah, Yom Kippur, Sukkot, Columbus Day, Navaratri, Halloween, All Saints' Day, Veterans Day, The Day Before Thanksgiving, Thanksgiving, Thanksgiving Weekend, or all of the month of December. Also not valid during work hours or blackout dates.

** Employee discount is limited to a one-time use only. Discount voucher not valid on toys, food, apparel, bedding, churros that aren't being used as food but are being used as—well, ask Mr. Franks—books, stationery, cold weather gear, hot weather gear, drinks, jewelry, Bacon Soup, or key chains.

BRINGING CHARACTERS TO LIFE

Anybody can pick up a pencil and create a cartoon character. Anybody! But it takes a special somebody—somebody with dreams—to make that character, well . . . *real*.

Bringing a character to life is about more than filming people in live action and then animating cartoons over their bodies to simulate realistic movement. It's about letting your pencil breathe, handing the reins over to your creation so they can have a hand in crafting their own stories.

Devotion to our characters—to capturing their stories—is why Joey Drew Studios exists at all. That, and dreams. Dreams, dreams, dreams. We hope you'll enjoy the closing pages of our employee manual, excerpted from *The Illusion of Living* by Joey Drew, his acclaimed memoir and guide to animation.

Joey Drew's Seven Rules
to
Animate By

When it comes down to it, there are seven rules that cartoon animations live or die by. Animators who follow these principles are able to achieve what we in the animation sphere call "the illusion of living" (that is, the illusion that your characters are real, living, breathing beings, with their own hopes, dreams, and desires).

Animators who succeed in achieving the illusion of living are of the highest caliber. Very few minds have been able to successfully crack the code. Thankfully, I, world-renowned and legendary animator Joey Drew, am here to guide you through those intimidating waters. In short, the seven rules to animate by are:

1. Your Animations Should Be Fluid
2. Your Animations Should (Mostly) Obey the Laws of Physics
3. Your Animations Should Control the Camera
4. Your Animations Should Be Aware of Their Environment
5. Your Animations Should Be Punctual
6. Your Animations Should Vary
7. Your Animations Should Haunt People

Rule #1:
Your Animations
Should Be Fluid

Think about a pail of water. When you carry the pail from one point to another, does the water inside stay perfectly still? Of course not! It sloshes about, spills over, ripples each time it's disturbed. Living bodies are made up largely of liquids, so your animations should have a level of fluidity to them.

Let's take a look at the cartoon character Bendy, for example. Bendy isn't exactly a liquid, but his body bounces with each footstep, his iconic smile dips a little before curving upward. Take note of the ripples in your body the next time you fall on your backside or clap your hands—these tiny details can take you far when trying to understand realistic movement.

When I first came onto the animation scene, most people were unaware of how to properly translate the fluid motions of everyday life onto the screen. By imitating the sloshing, stretching movements of water, I was able to take the first step to creating lifelike animations.

Rule #2:
Your Animations Should (Mostly) Obey the Laws of Physics

If you're like me, you fell asleep in your twelfth-grade physics lesson as soon as Mr. Junco started in on the math. But alas, physics—and the principle of physics—is highly important in animation.

Take Newton's First Law of Motion, for instance: An object at rest stays at rest, and an object in motion stays in motion, unless acted upon by an outside force. Now recall the juggling scene in the classic Bendy cartoon "Nightmare Circus":

-   Bendy looks down at the ball he rides and loses his balance
-   Bendy throws the last torch as he slips from the ball
-   Bendy lands on his back
-   The momentum causes him to do a flip, landing on his rear

    The momentum causes him to bounce once more after the fall

Bendy is in motion, speeding along on that ball at a good clip, until he's acted upon by an outside force: his own slip, followed by gravity. When he slips, he's not just going to fall to the ground. His momentum from his forward and downward motions has to go somewhere.

In animation, little exaggerations are okay and expected, so long as the rest of the motion is animated realistically. The flip Bendy does, for instance, is an exaggeration, but the little bounce that happens after the flip casts the illusion that Bendy really had enough momentum to not only flip, but even do one more bounce after that. Ensuring that these motions follow the laws of physics takes your animation from the realm of fantasy into reality.

IMPORTANT TIP: Pay attention to the *weight* of the items you are animating. A feather doesn't drop in the same way a sledgehammer or a book or a pie does.

Rule #3:
Your Animations Should
Control the Camera

Life is both the most boring and the most fascinating thing that exists. It's filled with exciting moments like chase scenes . . . and also with dull stretches of nothing, like waiting for a cab.

An animator who is hyperfocused on imitating real life will want to include those mundane moments: sifting through the kitchen pantry to find something to eat, selecting a can of chickpeas, draining the chickpeas, deciding those chickpeas aren't good enough to eat, and returning to the kitchen pantry to find something else. But even that was boring to read, wasn't it? No one wants to see *that* on the silver screen.

Properly done animations should control the camera, meaning they should be a highlight reel of the actions of the cartoon characters. They should strike the right balance between what's interesting and what's not to get to what's *real*. That doesn't mean your character should constantly be battling villains and racing across the city—that would get exhausting to watch.

Take our "Bacon Soup Bendy" cartoon; the entire short is focused on a hungry Bendy searching for something to eat. When he finally gets his moment of gratification at the end, our animators chose to pause here to illustrate each action: shaking the can, peeling back the lid, and finally, inserting the spoon to take a bite. This is because our animators were taking control of the camera, cutting out the unnecessary steps to get the soup and lingering on those satisfying moments of resolution.

Rule #4:
Your Animations Should Be Aware of Their Environment

In "The Butcher Gang," we had a lot of characters to manage. Usually it was just Bendy and Boris to look out for, but the Butcher Gang instantly doubled the number of characters we needed to animate. Yet how boring would this cartoon have looked if we only animated one character at a time, if none of the characters reacted to what was going on around them?

When Barley readies to throw the pie, you see each character being aware of their environment: Bendy cowers behind his tray, Edgar grins and ducks, and Charley leans forward incredulously when he realizes the pie is aimed in his direction. These characters are intensely aware of the actions going on around them, even Barley, who initiates the sequence by noticing and reaching for the pie on the counter. Your own animations must carry a similar level of awareness and depth.

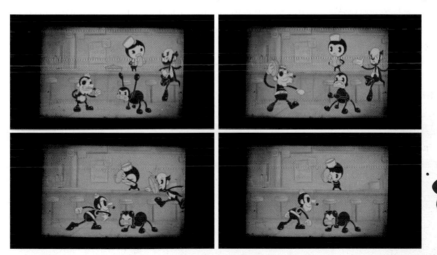

Who knew that something as simple as a pie-in-the-face gag would require so much thought to animate?

Rule #5:
Your Animations
Should Be Punctual

By this I mean your animations should have the proper timing—that is, things should happen in a sequence that makes sense and maximizes the potential of the story.

On the most basic level, this means making sure that Bendy bends his legs before crouching on the ground to pick up a carrot, that he rises up onto his tiptoes before placing the carrot properly, that he tilts his head to signal that he's making sure it's on right. These actions help the audience follow each movement in the sequence, to better help them understand what's going on in the scene.

In addition to having the proper sequential timing, your animations should also have timing that maximizes the storytelling potential, whether that potential is comedic or sorrowful or exciting.

After Bendy puts the finishing touches on his snowman, the sun comes up only to melt him away. Up to this point in the picture, the cartoon has been framed with Bendy at its center, so that the audience naturally follows him from start to finish. The audience has likely already forgotten about Boris the Wolf dropping his carrot.

At the last moment, Boris the Wolf saves the day with fantastic comedic timing. As the cartoon appears to have taken a sudden, sad turn, the wolf appears to relieve the sadness by picking up and munching on the carrot—classic Boris!

Rule #6:
Your Animations
Should Vary

When you storyboard out your animated feature, the kinds of cels you draw should vary. The bread and butter of the animation industry is a standard shot, framing only your necessary characters with minimal background. This shot is great for sequences, but sometimes showing close-ups can help audiences zero in on a character's reaction, while zooming out can show audiences how small and insignificant a character seems in the full scope of their environment.

We did many varying shots on our celebrated picture "Tombstone Picnic." Perhaps the most iconic shot in the piece is the wide shot of Bendy, whose visual relationship with a shadowy figure is shown in stark contrast by the framing and the scale. Varying cels like these add flavor and emotional depth to your animation.

Rule #7:
Your Animations
Should Haunt People

Ha-ha! This one is a joke—but not *entirely* a joke. Animations and cartoon characters that are fully realized and memorable are a different breed from your run-of-the-mill cartoon cat. How does one create cartoons that stick around long after that final shot? Well, if that isn't the million-dollar question . . .

One way to achieve this is to add little quirks to everything you draw. Give your main character an overbite, or a tic like touching his ear while talking. Look at the people around you—what quirks do they have that you can translate onto the page? These little side actions might seem like a waste of effort, but they make characters seem real, and thus easier to relate to.

Beyond the characters themselves, look at their clothes, their homes, their belongings. Every good actor makes use of the settings they're dropped into and the props that surround them. Think about what you can add to a character's surroundings that might say more about them. Is their home filled with junk? What do they have in their fridge? Are their clothes brand-new, or tattered and torn?

Breaking out of the sequence to dive into the finite details of the character will help ensure your characters haunt your viewers for years to come.

Animating Bendy

Bendy is our most beloved character here at Joey Drew Studios. As such, he has a strict model that all of our animators are asked to follow.

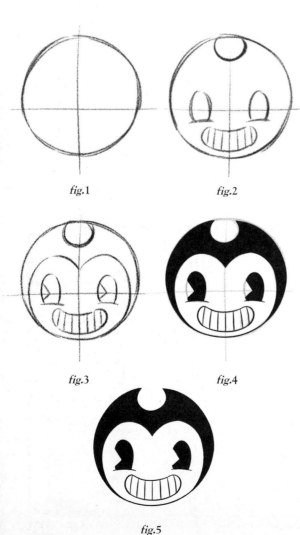

fig.1   fig.2

fig.3   fig.4

fig.5

1. Start by drawing Bendy in his largest, most basic shape: a circle. Draw a horizontal and vertical line through the center of the circle.

2. Draw another little circle at the very top of the first circle, for Bendy's horns. Along the horizontal line, at the midpoint between the left/right edges of the circle, draw Bendy's eyes, which look like an upside-down "U" with a line underneath them. Midway between the horizontal line and the bottom of the circle, draw Bendy's mouth. It's a sort of jelly-bean shape with seven lines for his eight teeth.

3. Draw a sort of half heart around Bendy's face. Cut out a small triangle from the left side of each of Bendy's eyes.

4. Shade in Bendy's eyes and the area around the heart shape of his face.

5. Erase your reference lines!

When animating Bendy, remember to keep these things in check:

-   Bendy's horns ALWAYS appear as pictured. It doesn't matter if Bendy is being featured from the side or the front. Bendy's horns are classic Bendy!

-   Bendy does NOT have a tail. Please do not animate Bendy with a tail.

-   Bendy also does not have a neck. His head floats on his shoulders.

-   Bendy does not have eyebrows; the heart shape of his face instead morphs to help convey different emotions.